The Silent Bride

THE SILENT BRIDE

WILLIAM C KINZLE

TENTH STREET PRESS

THIS EDITION

© Copyright 2013 William C Kinzle

Published by Tenth Street Press   2014

Original front cover image by Bayard Kurth
Cover design by Tenth Street Press

ISBN: 0-9923861-3-6

ISBN13: 978-0-9923861-3-9

PRINTED IN THE U.S.A.
TENTH STREET PRESS Ltd.
MELBOURNE LONDON
www.tenthstreetpress.com
Email:contact@tenthstreetpress.com

Chapter 1

Tony Brancusi bumped through a pothole and shot a glance sideways, unconsciously hoping to glimpse that wonderful milky ripple which always gave him such pleasure—even on TV. He had already cruised past his target twice, working up his nerve. It was shortly after 10:00 p.m. on a warm June evening, the time of year when twilight went on and on, deepening imperceptibly into pure black. Distant clouds bumped along to the north, and each breeze produced a ripple in the leaves of the poplar trees dividing the lots, sounding like a line of tall and skinny dancers discreetly shaking their tiny, tiny tambourines.

He dimmed his lights and slid to a stop a few doors down the street from a panel-sided one-story bungalow near the center of Vinewood, a formerly snazzy subdivision on Toledo's south side that had gone blue-collar 15 years ago. There were one or two weather-beaten 'For Sale' signs in each block, forlorn testimonials to the fact that nobody was buying here. People still kept the houses up, but standards had risen, and by those of today the area was pretty chintzy.

"Which house is it?" the woman asked, her voice automatically tough despite her nerves. She silently reassured herself that this would be okay.

Exhaling, Tony nodded at the one most in need of paint. It belonged to Bob Arkin, a former potential friend relegated to asshole jerkdom. Since the night of the poker game, just picturing his image filled Tony with a vindictive rage. He had gone out of his way to try to like the stupid moose, to overlook his inane gaffes at work, and how had his discreet advice been repaid? Stinging mockery, which Bob must have repeated to his friends, because suddenly everybody began looking at him differently.

"That one?" Now hints of trepidation were detectable in her voice.

Nodding, he looked around. "It'll go well," he said without thinking. What he didn't need was to be seen by someone sitting on their porch or putting out garbage. He lit a cigarette to help him relax—now he was anxious too. As an afterthought he held the Lucky up to her lips.

While he studied the street, she studied him. She put him at 36 to 40 years old, 190 pounds, maybe more. A softie. Smooth on the surface, but no doubt a temper underneath—she knew the type. Working the same job for the past ten years. No wedding ring, or tell-tale mark. She pictured a brief, early marriage to an unattractive woman who tried to mold him to her liking. Complaints led to yelling; the Mrs. would scream out of frustration at not getting through. Then a divorce. Recriminations to the friends. No children. He would have some nerdy hobby, like coin collecting or model trains. Subscribed to the Coin Collectors News. Still had the first issue.

"What's it like inside?" she wondered, letting the smoke drift out her nose.

It was like any other place, Tony told her. He'd been there three or four times, but everybody had been drinking. Details about room arrangement and furnishings were a blur. When he thought about the last poker game, all he could recall was how they'd insulted him. Especially the paunchy moron Bob. A real idiot playing for cheap laughs.

"He ain't no freak or nothin', is he? I should get more than a measly hundred bucks for this," she griped.

Tony knew it was good money for any of the women strutting their stuff near the ruins of the old train station. She had said fifty, probably would've settled for half, but he'd offered double, considering the unusual nature of his request.

"The tape runs for 45 minutes. Listen, you're gonna enjoy this," he told her, reaching out to pat her bare knee but stopping short. "Just relax and let it happen."

It was obvious that nobody was about, but second thoughts were keeping him from acting. Perhaps this wasn't such a good idea. What if it backfired? It might be better to just drive her back than to go any farther.

She sensed his faltering. Anxious for her money, she interrupted his reverie. "If we're gonna do it, let's fucking do it."

That made up his mind. Taking a deep breath, he stubbed out the smoke in the ashtray and opened his door. He came around to her side, and leaned into the car to apply her gag.

"C'mon, do I really have to wear this?" she griped.

"I explained it," he said, irritated. He put a perforated plastic ball in her mouth, and secured it with a piece of surgical tape from the roll in the glove compartment.

"Is that okay?" He didn't want to chance spoiling everything by having her suffocate.

She nodded, annoyed; what a clown. He fished a peel-off sticker from an envelope on the dash and removed the glossy tape on which gaudy red lips had been printed. Turning her head toward him, he carefully applied the stylized lips, knowing he could wreck the effect if he didn't get it right. They had been drawn slightly apart, as if the woman they represented were about to say something suggestive. The space between them was filled with layers of darkness, a close-up of a mysterious cave.

He had put an extra sticker on the front of his lav, opposite the can, to help him induce the context he needed for a transformative rapture.

Pulling back, Tony was satisfied with the job. "You look beautiful," he told her. "Now let me snap the player on, and we'll get started."

He took a small cassette player from the seat and fastened it around her neck with a strap. It hung against her chest, under her chin where it wouldn't get in the way. He grabbed a large poster-board placard from the back and leaned it against the side of the car.

"Let's go," he said, helping her out.

All she was wearing was a kind of flesh-colored spandex straight-jacket with circles cut out for her breasts. Her arms were crossed over her stomach, and the extended sleeves were fastened together behind her back with Velcro. With her long lashes and flashy make-up, the overall effect was of a queen of a futuristic porno movie. He looked at her for a long moment, tightening, pleased with his daring. He was really going to do this.

After reflexively smoothing his hair and tucking his shirt in by running his hand inside his trousers, he walked her quickly past the neighboring houses and up to Bob's door. She was unsteady in her high heels, probably because her arms were constrained. He carried the placard in his free hand—turned away from the street, just in case.

Once he'd positioned her square to the doorway he leaned the placard against her at an angle that would make it easy to read for Bob, who was six foot one or two. He moved it a little, checked the street again, and took a silk handkerchief from his pocket and tied it over her eyes.

Then he gave her some final advice: "Like I said, the last thing on the tape is a command to set you free. Once he does that, get out the door. Don't say any more than you absolutely have to, okay? I'll be waiting in the car with your clothes and your money. Be sure to bring the placard. You can fold it if you want to, but don't leave it behind. See you in 45 minutes."

He wanted to touch her, to reassure her, but he thought better of it. She knew what she was doing; she would be okay. She'd probably seen worse. He rammed the doorbell down for three seconds and then scooted around the corner of the house into a lush cedar hedge.

A moment later, Bob opened the door. He had thin hair, a moderate beer-gut, bushy eyebrows, and a rash on his chin from his morning shave; he had run out of shaving foam and tried using soap. He was wearing brown Hagar slacks and a mist-green Polo shirt, and holding both a can of Bud Lite and the sports section of the daily paper in his left hand. When he saw the woman, he visibly recoiled.

It took him a moment to comprehend the situation. Grinning as if he suspected he was on Candid Camera, he stepped past her and looked up and down the block. It was dark between the street lights. Across the pavement a cat appeared from alongside a garage and headed toward the Kool-aid stand that had been abandoned when the family next door left for a camping trip.

He returned to his doorway and looked her over. Her spandex suit stopped at her waist, exposing her magic triangle. The way she stood with her legs slightly apart made him swallow. He glanced up at her blindfold, and then back at the source of mystery. His eyes darted lower until they encountered the placard, which he took a moment to read:

Hi! Could you please help me? If you can, bring me inside, remove my blindfold, and turn this over and read the other side. If you can't, just close the door and I'll leave. Thank you very much.

She was about five five, five six. A tough type. She had short blonde hair, to which frosted streaks had been tastefully applied. A button nose, nice shape. She apparently took good care of her body, maybe working out on a stairmaster. She had a certain jauntiness, and seemed prettier than the women he knew.

After reading the message twice Bob scanned the street again. Finally he grabbed the placard, and cautiously pulled the woman inside, saying, "Well, okay, I'll bite." Once she was in, he released his grip on her and turned the placard over. The back side was printed in smaller block letters. He held it at arm's length, and read,

I've seen you around a few times since I got here from California, and I finally worked up my nerve. If you agree to help me play my favorite game, we can both have a lot of fun. Is that okay? Pretending I'm in danger really turns me on. So remember that my look is just part of the skit. If you're willing to go ahead with this, push the 'play' button on my recorder. I really appreciate this! Thank you very much.

Bob shifted through his gears. He examined the woman more closely, as if he might find clues. She was quite attractive, but the unusual circumstances made him hesitant. Suspecting that one of his coworkers at the TKD stamping plant was playing a joke, he put his beer and paper down, opened the door again, and looked around. There was still no discernible activity, except for the cat, which had swerved over to lick at a puddle. Shaking his head, Bob grinned and closed the door. The woman hadn't moved. Feeling awkward, he removed her blindfold and studied the placard again. He wanted to get this right.

The bozo grinning and moving his lips as he read seemed like a typical sap: soft, stupid, maybe unwittingly dangerous when he was acting out his weird fantasies, but she could handle him. She'd been to school on this kind of donkey.

She took a quick inventory of her surroundings. An open TV Guide on the overstuffed chair. A Tool Time re-run humming inanely across the room. A worn shag carpet with Doritos ground in. A framed print on the far wall of geese flying in front of a setting sun as hunters crouched behind the junipers. Typical crap. She should have asked for more dough.

Finishing the placard, he looked her over again. He noticed her clear green eyes, gaudy earrings, and the vaccination mark on her arm. She had a provocative natural stance. He guessed her age at 28. It was the kind of mistake that once had let her start drinking three years earlier than the law allowed, but now generally worked against her. She had cut the drunken oaf who had asked her to go home and send him her daughter.

Bob set the placard against the wall, reached over to grab the dangling recorder, and pushed 'play'. Then he stepped back. Almost instantly a woman's voice appeared, deep, sensual, and self-confident. "Thank you so much for agreeing to help me," it said, rippling with enticement. "I've gotten so this is the only thing that really excites me anymore. There's something basic about it. Primitive. Animalistic. Something that slices through the prohibitions we've been saddled with. I really appreciate it, and I'll do everything I can to make this as pleasurable for you as it will be for me."

There was a brief pause. The woman looked down toward the recorder, but her chin obscured the view. For a moment she was dumfounded at the voice coming from her chest: Tony hadn't told her what it would say. Suddenly she was paranoid, although considering everything she'd been through, paranoid wasn't the right word. Perhaps 'cheated', by not knowing what to expect. She shook her head, and tried to express her dislike of where she thought this was going by darting her eyes. But the message that Bob got was unclear, and the voice resumed its persuading before he could sort it out:

"You're a very handsome man. I'm lucky you aren't with someone else tonight."

"I could get a lot more dates if I was willing to play those games," Bob said gruffly. When that didn't sound exactly right, he added, "You know what I mean."

He was going to say more, but the cassette player interrupted him: "I may try to run away. That's part of my act. If I do, you should chase me, okay? When you catch me, you've got to punish me for being naughty. Put me over your knee, and spank me. Paddle me hard enough to bring a rosy glow to my skin. I like that. A good spanking makes me tingle. Sometimes I get off just from that! If you agree, look into my eyes and tell me what you'll do if I try to escape, okay? Go into the details, if you don't mind. It'll really help my fantasy if you put it into your own words, and make up a few things. I really appreciate this."

The voice was trusting, intimate, conspiratorial. After a brief hesitation, Bob complied. He positioned himself squarely in front of her, held her by the shoulders, and scrunched down to look into her eyes. "You should know that if you try to escape, I'll chase after you and catch you," he told her. He paused for a moment while he thought of how to continue. "I'll put you over my knee, and spank your butt," he said. "I'll pull your skin tight with one hand, and spank you good with the other." He was very earnest, but then he became worried about his performance and asked, "Is that okay?"

There was no reply. Thinking he was more of a boob than she'd expected, she tried to shake him off and pull away, but he gripped her more tightly. The taped voice took a mischievous, teasing tone: "You wouldn't really do that to me, would you? You're just saying you'll spank me, but I'll bet you really wouldn't."

"Oh, I'll do it all right," he replied, reaching down to adjust himself.

"You don't think my butt is too pretty for a spanking, do you?" the voice asked.

He regarded this as a trick question. "It's pretty, all right, but it could still use a good spanking," he said, proud of his rejoinder.

"Maybe you should spank me a little right now, just to show me that you mean business," the voice resumed. There was a noticeable increase in the speaker's breathing, and when the voice stopped, the breathing continued as an audible afterbuzz.

He was thinking that he'd heard about women like this.

The painted smile had been drawn with considerable precision. From some angles it seemed more real than her actual smile could have ever been. The lush color reminded him of the Vargas illustrations in the old Playboys he and his friends passed around. It suggested that despite her feigned agitation, she thought he was doing a good job.

"Just thinking about you spanking me is getting me all worked up," the voice added. "I can tell how warm your touch is going to make me feel. I'm sure you know what to do to a woman's butt, don't you. You're my idea of a real man."

Bob hesitated. He had never spanked a woman before. He knew it was sometimes done as a form of sex play. His friends had occasionally mentioned it. One night when they were intent on closing the bar, Luke, the layout man, had made a reference to the anchorwoman who'd come on TV spanking him: "I'd sure as hell let a broad like her paddle me!" And the video that Ed had shown when they were sitting around his apartment drinking beer after a Browns football game had contained a playful scene in which two girls took turns spanking each other. He had called that image back to mind several times since, although lately it wasn't as effective.

Bob wondered if he should take her into the bedroom to spank her, or do it right there. The woman's eyes had turned fiery, but when the voice came back, its calmness reassured him. "Do you think I'm good-looking? Turn me around, look me over. Touch me, okay? Don't be afraid. You can do anything you want to with me. I'm very proud of my features. All women like to be admired, you know."

The woman acted surprised, and resisted being turned. But she was no match for Bob, who outweighed her by a hundred pounds. He spun her around at arm's length so he could thoroughly evaluate her. She shook her head so violently that he wondered if he might not have turned her properly, so he did it again. "Don't you think I'm sexy?" the voice asked, its warmth swamping his doubts and re-establishing their complicity.

"You're very sexy," Bob awkwardly replied.

"That's sweet. Knowing you like me really turns me on. You really have a way with women that gets them hot just from how you look at them."

"You're the sexiest woman I ever met," Bob told her.

"I'll bet you've done this with a lot of women who are prettier than me," the voice remarked.

"No, I never did this before. Not exactly, I mean. And you're the prettiest, by far...."

"Would you lock the doors, just in case?" the voice urged. Bob took a moment to retrack himself before going over and locking the front door. "Turn the lights down, and put on some romantic music, okay? I want to really get in the mood."

"Do you like Neil Diamond?" Bob asked, turning on his stereo. Then he switched off the TV and dimmed the lighting.

"How about that spanking?" the voice said. "I'm getting hot just thinking about it."

His eyes glazed, Bob towed her over to the cloth couch. He sat down in the center, and pulled her onto him, twisting her so that her stomach rested on his lap. A song came on in which the singer crooned about his first love, a beauty in blue jeans. The song always made Bob imagine peeling them down, which would be difficult because they were so tight. Inch by inch, the luscious flesh would pop free.

Holding her steady, he put his hand in the small of her back and pressed on the area where her extended sleeves were fastened. The effect of his pressure was to push her haunches up, as if her flesh were issuing an invitation. He ran his other hand over her, back and forth, testing, measuring, amazed at her perfection. Beneath her skin her muscles had a kind of resilience that made them respond to his motion. It was as if they pushed back, encouraging him. Fascinated, he rubbed her with a little more strength. Her muscles rippled like currents in a bowl of jello.

"Ooh, I really really like this," the voice said.

After awhile, he stopped rubbing, raised his hand, and gave her a tentative slap. It produced an intriguing bounce. She turned her face sideways, trying to rise, and kicked futilely in the air. The fluttering of her strapped-on high heels added to her enticement. He held her securely, and slapped her again. Responding to the slap, the voice told him in throaty tones, "Oh, thank you, thank you, I need this so very much! You understand women so well! You know I deserve this, too, don't you, because I've been thinking naughty things. You like doing this, don't you? Or don't you? Maybe you're only doing this to be nice to me. If that's the case, I really owe you for this."

He slapped her with a little more strength. Her flesh quivered with his touch, so he slapped her again. The voice moaned sensually, urging him not to stop. It was building toward a crescendo. He knew, abstractly, that the voice wasn't exactly her speaking, but just as the characters played by good actors become real on stage, it seemed to him that the woman he was spanking was somehow speaking to him through the tape. When she twisted her head so she could look at him, the seductive painted smile reinforced the illusion. Slapping harder, he started talking to her, telling her that he was doing this as a special favor because he knew how much she liked it, and wanted it, and needed it. He meant it with all his heart.

The voice encouraged him, chanting, "Oh, God, oh God how I love this, oh God damn. I need this to be a real woman! Oh God this is good!"

He no longer waited for a pause to speak. Instead he started a monologue that fed on the taped voice, repeating its phrases, altering them and blending them together. "You love this, don't you," he murmured huskily. "You need this. It's making you into a complete woman. It feels so God-damn good." Glycerin was oozing from the spigot.

He paused. Not having meant to swear, he corrected himself —"it feels very good"— and continued.

The flesh under his slapping reddened, as did his face. Sweating now, he pressed on her back harder than he intended, making her arch up to meet his descending hand. He pressed down again with his left hand to force her haunches up just as he slapped her. Then he eased up to let her sink back down, establishing a rhythm. He began rocking, and his eyes developed a sheen. He blabbered along with the tape in extended, run-on sentences. The couch was banging against the wall, knocking into the plaster so that dust and powdery crumbs were accumulating on the floor. The constantly teasing voice was taking him past all control.

He tightened as a warm sweetness began seeping into his legs. It started at his knees, inflaming his thighs as it rose. He slapped and rocked with unfettered force, pressing and releasing to encourage a point of intense pleasure that made its inevitable appearance. It expanded quickly, dominating his receding perceptions until it exploded in all directions. As it faded, he was left panting. He could feel the wetness cool. After another moment, he realized he had come to rest.

He leaned back and closed his eyes. The tape was silent, but after awhile the voice returned, speaking in a satisfied and grateful tone: "Thank you so very much. I'll never be able to tell you how good that made me feel. When you're up to it, sit me on your lap, okay? I have another favor to ask."

He pulled her around so she was sitting on his lap.

"Tell me that I have to do everything that you ask me to. Otherwise, you'll spank me again. Say that if I don't completely obey, you'll get a spatula or something to tan my fanny with real good. Tell me it might leave some welts that'll turn into ugly scars. No woman wants her ass damaged, because that's what we use to get a man's attention. Not that I have to explain that to you. I can tell you've really figured out women. Order me to nod if I agree to obey you."

"I want you to do exactly what I say," Bob muttered, his eyes not quite focusing. A momentary thought came to him of going into the bathroom to wipe off, but then it flickered away. "If you don't do what I say," he chanted,

"I'll have to really tear into you. You won't be able to sit down for days. It might leave scars on your beautiful backside. You don't want that, do you? Nod if you'll do what I say."

Affronted, she shook her head angrily. This was more than she'd bargained for: she should've known better than to trust a creep like Tony. When she saw him again, she resolved to stick him for treating her with such disrespect. If she ever saw him again—the chances of him waiting around outside had to be nil.

She felt she'd be damned if she'd let this blubbery oaf continue, but when he started to pull her back over his knees she reversed herself and nodded. Tony had said 45 minutes. The tape had to be about half over, she reasoned, unless that was another lie. He interpreted the distraction in her eyes as longing, and fondly rubbed her thigh.

Then the voice said, "There's something I want you to command me to do, but I'm a little shy. Maybe it'd help me get in the right mood if you'd lick my nipples. Would you do that for me, as a special favor? Make 'em stand out, stiff and hard. I know you're good at this, and I'll really appreciate your work."

He started to answer, but his words were choked off by emotion. So he clumsily bent over, and kissed and rubbed her breasts, caressing first one and then the other, licking her nipples and squeezing them between his stubby index finger and broad, flat thumb. He began to work them harder while he slobbered over her shoulder and neck, melting into a thick, warm passion. The voice reassured him, breathlessly telling him he had a wonderful touch and pleading with him not to stop.

"It's not right that I'm naked, but you still have your pants on," the voice teased a moment later. "That's not fair, is it?"

"That's not fair," Bob answered.

"Why don't you take them off. I'll bet you're a big, handsome guy."

Bob unbuckled, unsnapped, and unzipped, and then rose up enough to slide out of his slacks. Shy, he hoped she wouldn't look at the stains on his boxers.

"Oh, you're quite a man, I can see that. You've got the kind of equipment I really love. Not so big that you'll hurt, but built just right for a sensitive woman like me."

A resurgence of strength was giving him new life.

"You've made my nipples feel fantastic. You're really invigorating me. Your touch is so hot and sensual. But I feel a little top-heavy. Why don't you ask me if I want you to rub me somewhere else, lower down? Tell me that if I don't nod yes, you'll have to spank me really hard, and maybe even get a stick. You're quite an expert at this, by the way. Any woman would go out of her mind to have you treat her like this. Please don't stop until I come again, okay? God, I can't believe how good you are at training me!"

"D'you want me to rub you lower down? You know you'll like it. You might as well agree, because if you don't, I'll just have to spank you until you change your mind."

Her eyes became distant, as though she were focusing on being somewhere else. She'd stopped thrashing, but she couldn't bring herself to nod. He was caught up in the routine, though, and didn't notice. Instead, he pried her legs apart, touched his lips, and brought his moistened hand toward the forbidden place.

"Oh, God, this is like electricity!" the voice exclaimed, even before he applied the lacy foam. It was followed by a moan that tickled the back of his neck. The sequence the groan described was a little out of synch, but the meaning was clear.

He threw a leg over one of hers to pry her farther apart, and prodded her with his fingers. He licked his hand, and let her see the moisture he had struggled to generate. The voice urging him on no longer spoke in complete sentences. When it asked him to tell her how long he'd wanted to do this, he began a litany that blended obscure fantasies with the current situation. A fresh drop of goo appeared on his tip.

The voice pleaded with him to give her what she needed. He only had to pull her a little way over in order to enter. He was surprised at her tightness, despite all his work. Then she gloved him, and he was in a different world.

William C Kinzle

"Oh, God, this is wonderful!" the voice moaned. "Oh God, shit! Jesus, oh, oh, oooh!" In response, he bucked roughly up and down, holding her tightly. The couch smashed into the wall, raising clouds of fine white dust that set his mind swirling with the excitement of the situation as he breathed them into his lungs. She entreated him not to stop. He couldn't see her face, but he knew she was deeply enraptured.

Once again the throe started in his thighs, the glow from a distant light that was zooming into the foreground like a comet on a rendezvous with Earth. At first he fought against it, but it slipped through his defenses as effortlessly as water through a sieve. Just like that it was behind his barricades and in his brain, and a wake of ecstasy erupted like the flow of life itself, a fountain of pleasure encouraged by the voice assuring him that this was so very, very good.

He felt that now the memory of the women from the bars he went to after work could be consigned to the scrap heap. They had been so difficult to satisfy, and had always demanded things afterward. Now he had turned the corner on that. Floating toward a warm nook on the spent gust of a breeze, he was already anticipating the joy that remembering this would bring.

After awhile he lifted her off him and sat her at his side. He was no longer panting. He grabbed a tissue from the box sitting on the stack of Penthouses on the end-table, and wiped himself. Not thinking, he sniffed the wadded-up tissue before dropping it behind the couch. The voice returned, assuring him, "That was the best I ever had. I'll never, ever forget it."

He drifted off for awhile. Then he stood up, grabbed his pants, and headed for the bathroom. "Was it anywhere near as good for you as it was for me?" the voice asked behind him.

He turned to answer, noticing that one of the tapered wooden legs had broken off the couch. "Even better," he told her, but instead of acknowledging his answer, she stared dumbly around the room. Anywhere but at him.

After washing himself in the bathroom, he put his pants on and headed for the kitchen to get himself a beer. He heard her ask him something, though, so he forsook his refreshment and returned to the living room. He pulled her to her feet, and then dabbed at the sweat on her brow with another tissue. Her body had become a bellows to facilitate her rough, fitful breathing.

She had the shell-shocked expression he associated with the consummation of passion. "I should make you spank me until I admit what a terrible slut I am," the voice said playfully. The woman's eyes showed signs of fresh panic, but her tone was one used between special friends. "I can't ever get enough of a real man like you. But I've got to go. Would you release the Velcro strip behind my back? My girlfriend's gonna meet me down the street in a few minutes, okay? I can't wait to tell her how good this was. Maybe she'll want to come see you next."

He wasn't sure what to do, but the woman's stern

expression helped him decide. As soon as he freed her arms, she peeled the tape off her lips and spit out the ball. Holding back the urge to punch him, she became business-like. Grabbing the placard, she hurried out the door.

Outside in the cool night air, she had a moment of doubt, but Tony was there to meet her on the neighbor's lawn. He took the placard, and helped her to the car. As soon as they were in, he helped her out of the costume. She shook off his clumsy attempt at helping her dress and began to complain. "Jesus H. Christ! That was a lot fuckin' weirder than you said!"

"What happened?" he shot back, unsnapping the cassette player and throwing it on the back seat. "Nothing went wrong, did it? Did he buy it? How did it go?"

"I'm just sayin' it was fuckin' weird! I shoulda got twice."

Chapter 2

Inside the bungalow, Bob popped open a beer and sat down to think over what had just happened. Between sips he glanced around the room, reacquainting himself with the normal surroundings. He was breathing heavily from the confluence of emotions: mystification, lingering excitement, and a sense that he should feel guilty, even though he wasn't sure why.

He replayed the experience in his mind, finding no reason to fault himself. Nodding to ratify his good feeling, he finished his beer and got another.

He had a hard time believing it had really occurred. He went to the door and looked outside, as if something there might prove his memory. But the street was lifelessly quiet, as usual. Shaking his head, he went back in and sat down by the phone.

Feeling he had to talk to someone about his experience, he dialed his friend Ray Cronin, a co-worker at TKD who lived in Shakerton Village, the next suburb to the east. "What're you doin'?" he asked him, fighting to stay calm.

"Thinkin' about goin' to bed," Ray replied. "The fuckin' Indians lost another one. They got the bats but their relievers all have dead arms. Honestly, how anyone could give those mopes that kinda money's beyond me." As he spoke, he sensed his friend's excitement.

"Don't turn in yet. I'm comin' over. I want to tell you about something amazing that just happened."

"Well pick up a 12-pack. I'm all out of beer."

It took Bob 15 minutes to reach Ray's house, which was similar to his own except it was turned 90° to present a gable to the street and had plastic shutters flanking the square windows. There was a two-stall garage built on the side, where the two long-time friends had fixed a motorcycle and half a dozen cars.

Ray took two Buds out and put the rest of the 12-pack in the fridge. They sat down on stools at the elbow of the counter, and Bob told him his story out of sequence, going over some parts two or three times.

"Holy shit!" Ray burst out, shaking his head. "You're sure you're not makin' this up?"

"I swear, it happened just like I'm saying! She was from California," he added. "That must be where she developed a taste for kinky stuff."

"Who was she?"

"I don't have any idea! I never saw her before, and she didn't say a word, except for what was on the tape."

"What did she look like?"

"She was a real dish!"

"And you screwed her?"

"What've I been telling you! I had no choice. It was like I got hypnotized by how strange it was, or something. Not that I wouldn't a done it anyway. I was gonna do it again, except she had to go."

"I gotta ask. Was it any good?"

"Damn straight! Of course, I haven't been getting much since the divorce. But she was a hell of a lot better than Gladys ever was, by God. I couldn't have said no if the house caught on fire. She knew what to do!"

"I mean for her."

It took Bob a minute to realize his friend was joking.

"Did she really get off on the weird stuff?" Ray asked.

"I guess. She seemed to. But how d'you ever really know?"

Grinning, Ray got them each another beer. "You had to spank her, first?" he asked. He wanted Bob to tell him again. And again.

"That's what she wanted," Bob said. "She really liked it. And her butt really liked it. It kept asking for more."

"Huh?"

"You know, in the way it turned rosy and warm."

"And you didn't have to pay her or anything?"

31

"No! Afterwards she just took off. Never said nothin' about money. She just used me to screw her. It was like she needed a good cock, and I happened to be there."

"God damn you're a lucky son of a bitch!"

They continued to talk about Bob's encounter until the beer was gone. Under Ray's prodding, Bob recited all the details again.

Ray asked a number of questions Bob could not answer. He didn't know if it was the woman's own voice on the tape, or how she'd chosen him, or how to reach her if he wanted to help her out again. "Jesus Christ, man, you shoulda phoned me to come over before you let her go! God damn it," Ray complained. "I mean, what are friends for?"

When they finished off the 12-pack Ray brought another in from the garage and asked Bob o tell him the whole story again.

A mile away in Tony's car the woman, Gina, stretched her arms and rotated her hands to restore her diminished circulation. She too was full of questions, which she asked Tony as he drove her back downtown. How did he ever come up with such a trippy bit? Had he done this before? Who had made the tape for him? Was the walrus that she'd screwed really in on it; was he the one who had put up the hundred bucks to hire a girl to act out his fantasy?

Tony glanced at her and grinned each time she asked

him something, but didn't answer. She didn't seem to mind; she was just sort of thinking out loud.

"There wasn't a hidden camera or nothin', was there? I mean, I'd be pissed if I turned on the cable station some night, and saw myself in a straight-jacket getting poked by that guy."

He assured her there hadn't been any cameras.

"'Cause I get extra for that, you know. Hey, he shot a wad into his underpants from spankin' me," she told him. "But I suppose you figured on that. That's why the broad on the tape told him to do it, right?"

Tony continued grinning, but didn't reply.

"I guess I'm lucky he wasn't the type to get off from peein' on me. Or doin' any freaky stuff."

"You want me to take you home, or drop you back on the street?" Tony asked.

"Back on the street. My night's just begun."

When he reached her regular place he pulled over to let her out. She opened the door, but turned to him with a last question. "What would you say if I told you I memorized the guy's phone number so I could call him and make my own deal to do it again?"

Getting a grip on his sudden panic, he tried a bluff that he'd seen on TV: "Lady, you screw with me and you'll wind up at the bottom of Lake Erie!"

His voice broke, though, and she could tell he didn't mean it. All in all, she thought he wasn't such a bad guy. After all, he had paid her. "I was just kiddin'," she said, getting out in front of a closed-down drug store. "Can't you take a joke? Anyway, you know where to find me if you need me again."

Her real name was Sherri Litwak, but everyone on the street knew her as Gina. She was 25, only dabbled in drugs, and had been married twice: once, when she was 15, to a sailor on leave who had taken her to Las Vegas for a week and then disappeared when he sobered up. She later heard he was killed in a freak accident, but she didn't bother applying for his benefits. Too much red tape. She married again, 8 years later, despite the promise she had made to herself.

She had been living in Detroit, working as a waitress at an all-night bowling alley where the local sports and music personalities hung around. Things were going along okay. She was putting money aside, having fun, not taking anything too seriously. Until the arrest.

It was some kind of sting. She and three black jocks and a woman she had recently met named Sheila were snagged sniffing coke, naked, in a room at the Holiday Inn. Just when she was cruising, seven clouds up. Sheila had urged them to score, and had talked Big Leon out of going home early. She turned out to be the vice cop. In the interview, Sherri told Detective Litwak how she'd been set up. It was okay; the cops just wanted her to testify against Big Leon. He was too damn smug for his own good. After all, he had lost his starting job on the

Lions' defensive line and wasn't likely to get it back. He should have acknowledged his betters. It would have been cheaper.

Crossing her fingers, she said yes.

The detective took pity on her. She seemed like a nice kid. Driving her home, he told her how he had nine years to go for his pension, and then it was winters in Tallahassee, fishing and golf. He had been married twice, and had sworn off. Every so often he had to take a second job doing security to catch up on his alimony. Luckily, jobs like that were always available. Sometimes with benefits.

They stopped at a Flapjack Shack for breakfast. His name was Gus. He was a hockey fan, as was she. He complained that neither of his sons had any interest. He hardly ever saw them, except on the court's ridiculous schedule. Their mother, his first wife Marge, spoiled them, making them flabby and hostile to him when he made his monthly visit. The second wife —well, all he would say about her was that anyone can be fooled.

Looking at him, she saw he had a susceptibility that matched her power. He would be easy for her to control, almost second nature. What the heck, she told herself, I might as well go out with him. After what she'd been through she reasoned that having a cop on the string could come in handy.

Surprisingly, they hit it off. He acted like a kindly uncle. She liked that; it negated the memory of her Uncle

Benny, who had caught her in a weak moment and then used that to blackmail her until she left home.

Gus didn't believe in a long courtship. "If you're gonna do something, then you oughta do it. Besides, I could be dead tomorrow." Four months later, Sherri Antieul became Sherri Litwak in a private ceremony at City Hall.

It was a good life for awhile. The humdrum routine helped her get her head back together. Sometimes Gus became sloppy when he drank, but never mean. Pitiful was more like it. He was a good-hearted guy. Some of his vice cases got him worked up in the telling, and she was savvy enough to act out those roles. After all, it was something to do.

Hockey was the love of his life. He enjoyed having his buddies over to watch the games on TV. Sometimes they brought a girlfriend. Never wives. They liked to mystify women with hockey jargon, which she pretended not to grasp. They enjoyed patiently explaining the game's intricacies. A couple of them patted her in a way that was only half friendly.

One afternoon Lieutenant Spezio called her at home. Gus had introduced them at a cop bar. He was handsome, although not as much as he imagined. He had a devil-may-care attitude, and acted like he could handle whatever came up.

One day he phoned her and said he was running a sting at the airport, and Sheila had come down with something. "Some bug. She'll be okay tomorrow, but our chance to grab this goon's right now. If you could get him to score some coke for you, make a call and have it delivered to a hotel room, you know, we'll make it worth your while. Only take you an hour, maybe less."

She protested. "Jesus, Rich, I don't have the clothes for that!"

"Hell, we got an entire wardrobe down here."

"Is Gus part of this?"

"Gus who?"

It went smoothly. Lieutenant Spezio put in a voucher for her for $200, plus she could keep what she got from the mark—another $350. Spezio drove her home, thanked her, and told her there might be a chance to do it again, if she'd like. "You're much better than Sheila."

"Would Gus have to know?"

"I'll leave that up to you."

Everything went along fine for the next few months. She was making about $1000 a week, free money. The men Spezio's team wanted to bust were completely predictable: arrogant losers who would do anything to impress a new woman. She began to take pride in helping get them off the street.

When Gus got suspicious of what she was buying she told him she had gotten a job. One of her old buddies agreed to cover for her. When the friend began to insinuate that his help ought to be worth something, she mentioned it to Spezio, and he stopped by and set the man straight.

It went bad all at once. The team had been after a low-life named Randy Terkel for months. He was in and out of town, which made it tricky. On this trip he had been there for three days, during which they followed him everywhere. Finally he relaxed after some big score, tying one on in the Bull's Balls, a hang-out for wise-guy wannabes.

She had just started having a quick one with Spezio on the way home. It was the best way to unwind, plus he was hung like a stallion. He took pride in showing her tricks he thought her drab older husband wouldn't know. When he called, her anticipation of another session gave the operation an added glow, which the marks picked up on. She changed into one of the outfits she'd acquired, hopped into the Miata she had told Gus was part of her inheritance from an imaginary aunt, and headed for the steak house at 2:00 in the afternoon.

She entered in a way designed to get Terkel's attention. He noticed, sent her a drink, and then asked her to join him in his booth. When she purred about coke, he called someone who promised to be there in ten minutes.

Unfortunately, the connection turned out to be Billy Bryan, whom she had set up a month before. Spezio had told her he would be sent away, but the evidence had gotten fouled up and Bryan was still walking around. Spezio had been too embarrassed to mention it, and figured that in a city of a million people, what were the odds?

As soon as Bryan saw her, though, he told Terkel it was a sting. Terkel, a short, almost runty man with ratty features and a bad complexion, took it personally. After the way he'd been letting her pocket the change when he paid for their drinks with hundred dollar bills, he felt unpardonably betrayed. Terkel decided to cut her good, right there in the restaurant.

Figuring the cops were close by, Bryan tried to stop him. But Terkel was a man possessed. Refusing to listen to reason, he slashed Bryan across the belly, and then lunged for Sherri. She was trying to stand, and his blade hit her thick leather belt. As he recoiled for a second blow, the team rushed in, disarmed him, broke his teeth, and took him off to jail. Spezio comforted his distraught operative, who had never had such a close call before. In shock, she leaned into his strong chest, unable to stop crying. Neither of them noticed the cop who had been trailing Bryan, who had come in behind him and was sitting hunched over in the corner, watching events unfold.

Gus bided his time, investigating the depths of her calumny and considering appropriate ways to get his revenge. He considered alerting Spezio's current target, a real psychopath, and letting him mete out justice, but he really wanted to be there himself when it happened.

He began following Sherri when he knew Spezio had something going. He wasn't sure what to do, and hoped that circumstances would tell him when the time was right. In the meantime, their home life was going to hell. He became sullen and untalkative. She was getting so caught up in the life that she barely noticed, and didn't have the patience to draw him out.

Finally, on a day when he had tailed his wife back from another small-time bust to a seedy room at the High-Hat Motel on Woodward Avenue, he felt he just couldn't wait any longer. After screwing on his silencer, he kicked down the flimsy door and went in firing. Luckily for her she happened to be in the bathroom, strapping on a different pink appliance. Unluckily for Gus, the man he filled full of lead wasn't the marginal Spezio but the rotund Assistant Chief of Police Vincent Vandelay, a man of considerable political clout.

When she came out of the bathroom in her lacy black harness with the obscene horn, the full weight of what he'd done was just settling into him. He barely recognized her. He'd entered a place where everything was eerie and unfamiliar. He saw himself imprisoned like a common criminal, harassed, tortured. He put the gun to his forehead, but was stopped by her disdainful comment: "Jesus Christ, what's done is done! Grow up, don't be a fuckin' weenie."

It was enough to ignite his smoldering rage. He pointed the gun at her, telling himself that another body wouldn't hurt. He started to squeeze the trigger. She lowered her head sharply and gave him the look that always transformed his resolution into confusion and lust. She had no doubt she could control him, even under these circumstances, and she was right. Bit by bit, his gun began to wilt.

Glaring, she grabbed her dress and swooped past, glad she'd been relieved of having to do Vandelay—screw Spezio's promotion. By the time Gus came to his senses and drove home she had cleaned out her things and stopped at both of her banks on the way out of town.

The money had run out in Florida. She started working her way north, learning about new worlds on the way. That had led to her frequent remark, "Jesus, maybe I should write a God-damn book, tell people what's really goin' on!" She'd actually started one once, setting up chapters in a spiral notebook for each of the unusual things that seemed to give men so much pleasure. But seeing her name on the lined tablet had made her apprehensive, and she tore out the pages she had filled and burned them in the sink. Besides, she didn't know how to spell.

She was drawn back to Detroit, but she refused to admit it. Stopping in Toledo, she promised herself, "This far, and no farther," although she sometimes thought about driving up to see her old neighborhood. She wondered if visiting the places where she'd been an entirely different person might close the circle in which she was spinning, and allow her to move on to the next stage, whatever that turned out to be.

Now she was back on the street, watching Tony's taillights depart. She stood for a while at her regular spot, but her heart wasn't into doing any more business. When a car that had cruised by several times slowed and stopped, and the power window descended and a middle-aged man's scratchy voice called out pathetically, "Hey, Gina," she didn't bother going over to it to conduct the usual negotiation. Instead she started ambling down the block, hoping to find her friend Rose.

Gina's spot was in front of a boarded-up pharmacy, which she had chosen because of the implication of health conveyed by the faded ads for various medications still taped to the inside of the plate glass windows. Rose had chosen the glamour of a closed-down fur store in the next block, whose bare mannequins suggested to passers-by that with a little imagination women could be posed in a variety of interesting and unusual positions—and animated through the flow of crisp new bills.

Rose, in skin-tight short shorts and three-inch spike-heeled boots, was just getting out of a large dark car as Gina approached. Rose leaned in and swore a blue streak before slamming the door, and then straightened her short skirt as the car hurried away. Approaching her, Gina heard the torrent of curses but also caught Rose's smile, which indicated the profanity was probably just the final part of the game.

Rose was a redhead in her late 30s, taller and thinner than Gina. At the moment she was drug-free, but she lived one day at a time and had no idea what tomorrow might bring. Primarily she felt lucky to have maintained custody of her daughter Angel, who was already ten. Or was it eleven? Gina liked her because she was sympathetic, fairly intelligent, and had a good sense of humor. She took things as they came, always found the irony in life, and made a good confidant.

"You'll never guess what happened to me," Gina began as she drew close to her friend.

"It can't be any weirder than what happened to me," Rose replied.

Thinking her own story would take longer, Gina decided to let Rose go first, to get her tale out of the way. "Tell me about it," she said.

Rose did. Delighted at being annoyed, she related how her date had driven her out to his home on Evergreen on the city's east side, where he'd had an altar set up for a funeral in his dank basement. He had made her wait in the foyer while he went in first, changed into a tux, and climbed into a fancy coffin. When she heard the organ music start, she and solemnly entered the candle-lit room, as he had instructed.

The light had been rosy and low. Red and purple velvet sashes adorned the walls. Her date had recorded a eulogy to himself, which was playing when she came in. He'd carefully explained what she was to do: "When they say I was a good man, an upright father and husband, a helpful member of the community, you deny it, okay? You say that you knew all my dirty little

43

secrets, and the opposite was more like the truth."

He'd told her to make up examples. Anything that came to her mind, the dirtier, the better. "If I haven't done it, I'm sure I wanted to. And that's just as much of a sin," he had said.

She had thrown herself into her performance, as usual. Whatever claims the eulogy made—his church work, helping with the Scouts, support of various charities—she had countered with examples of how he had wallowed in one or another sleazy perversion. She was so convincing that she began to believe it herself. After all, he was a man.

"That doesn't sound so bad," Gina offered.

"Let me tell you! That part was okay, but after awhile I noticed that his cock was jutting straight up. Here he was, lying in a coffin with his eyes closed, dressed in black and with his face powdered white, and his cock was twitching like an epileptic on the verge of a seizure. I thought he probably wanted to be yanked off or something, so I reached over and grabbed him. Boy was that a mistake! He just about went through the roof. He sat bolt upright and started screamin', 'I never told you to do that! Now you've ruined everything!' So he drove me back here in total silence and refused to pay me a dime."

So her stream of expletives had not been an act.

"You gonna put out his name?" Gina asked, referring to some of the guys they knew who tried to impress them by offering to take care of any problem that came up.

"Naw, I don't think so. The poor sap's just crazy. So, what happened to you, girl?"

"Let's get some coffee," Gina replied. "It's a long story."

Some of the other street girls taking a break in Wendell's nodded or said hello when Gina and Rose entered the coffee shop. With its pastel mural of a country scene with groupings of Victorian society in fancy finery wrapped around the walls, it radiated a fairy-tale aura that heightened their sense of refuge. Sammi was there in her trademark outfit of satin pants, white linen shirt, and man's multicolored tie, catching up on the gossip. She was married now, but she came down one or two times a week to chat with her friends after her wealthy new husband fell asleep. There was Trixie, who had just gotten out of the hospital and wasn't strong enough to work yet. And mousy Leona, whose teeth were rotting from lack of care. Rose had told her that she had bad breath but it hadn't phased her: "It ain't like I'm gonna kiss 'em. What they got in mind, they'll never know."

Passing on an invitation to join the Waddle Sisters, two immense, happy-go-lucky women in their mid-thirties who joyously handled the heavy trade, Gina and Rose took a booth by themselves toward the back. When the waitress came around the counter to take their order they asked for just coffee.

Once she left, Gina told Rose what had happened. It was a two-refill story. "The guy really got turned on," she concluded.

"Girl, that was dangerous," Rose declared. "That tape coulda said anything."

"Yes, but people can say anything, too," Gina replied. "I mean, nice guys can suddenly turn ugly. So what's the big deal? Besides, it didn't feel dangerous."

"Don't tell me you found it exciting," Rose said. "You always did get off on the crazy stuff."

"I don't know. I was a little tense at first because I had no idea what might be next. I suppose it could've been dangerous. But it was also like Days of Our Lives, you know? I mean, it was like watchin' a soap opera, only I was in it."

"What could you have done if it had turned bad?"

"Not much, really. Kicked the window out, maybe. The strap was Velcro, so I might have caught it on a table edge or something and peeled it back. But the thing was, this guy was like hypnotized by the voice on the tape. I had the feeling I was just watching him act out his fantasy. I didn't have to worry about what to do at the right time or anything, either, because the voice on the tape was in control. It was kind of relaxing for a change."

"Relaxing! Hah! I'm just glad it didn't happen to me. I get claustrophobic whenever a guy wants to tie me up. I always tell him, 'You first.' You'd be surprised how many jerks really want that anyway."

"I think it might be okay if you'd hear the tape beforehand. So you knew just what was gonna happen."

A car pulled up outside the restaurant and honked. Sammi called to Rose, "Hey, it's one of your regulars." Then, when Rose flounced outside to see him, Sammi came back to have a cup with Gina.

Gina wasn't done talking her experience out of her system. "Let me tell you what happened to me," she started in again. Sammi was all ears, responding to her friend with emotional bursts at the appropriate points to keep the story going. Hearing these vignettes put a little excitement in her life.

When Gina finished, Sammi repaid her enthusiastic rendition with a gush of appreciation: "Christ, Gina, if things like that had happened to me, I wouldn't have retired!"

"I don't know who the dufus was, but he seemed to really get off on it," Gina insisted. "I mean it." She added the qualifier, because she knew how often the girls made this claim. "And the best thing was, I didn't have to work so damn hard. In most cases you gotta be absolutely sure you stay on theme, you know? One wrong move, one unguarded expression, and the jerk'll go limp. When that happens they always keep their money."

47

"Never happened with me, girl."

Gina gave her a three-second stare. "Me either. I'm just saying. Anyway, this time I felt I could relax and let it spin out. There wasn't anything I could do. If something went wrong, it wouldn't be my fault for once."

They were joined by Midget, a pale, nervous man in his 40s who stood five foot three. His nickname rankled him because he suspected it referred to a lack of intelligence or moral sensibility more than stature. They tolerated him because he came up with more than his share of entertaining ideas, but they didn't trust him because if one of them even looked like it might pay off he would go back on his word or reconfigure the situation to get a bigger share of whatever might be gained.

Sammi paved the way for Gina to tell her story again: "Hey, Midget, you gotta hear what happened to her!"

"Okay," Midget said, sitting next to Sammi. He stubbed out his cigarette and offered his pack around before lighting another. He was thin and small-boned, with sallow cheeks, and a prominent nose. His black hair occasionally fell over his forehead and had to be thrown back. At times he seemed surprisingly smart, but then he would belay that impression by taking out a jackknife and cleaning his nails while he was talking, oblivious to how repulsive it was.

Gina related what had happened to her again, leaving

out the details she felt she'd told enough. Midget hung on her every word, obviously caught up in the unusual event. When she was done Sammi rapped his arm and said, "I told you, didn't I? What d'you think of that?"

"Holy Christ in a Hoover!" Midget exclaimed, exhaling his words in a puff of smoke. His left eyelid executed a dazzling flutter. Sammi glanced at Gina, as if she should be acknowledged for having known Midget would be impressed.

"It wasn't too bad," Gina apprised.

"We were just sayin' that a girl don't have to be so nervous about how a customer's doin' with this kind of deal, because it ain't her responsibility," Sammi said. "The guy shot such a wad he could have put a hole in his own damn ceiling!"

"Too bad you couldn't of kept the tape," Midget said. "We could set up our own business with it."

"Huh?" Gina asked.

Sammi's eyes lit up, as though she felt Midget was onto something. "Sure. You liked it, didn't you? And the guy really got off," she chimed in. "Maybe you could try running the same deal for other customers."

"Everybody needs an edge," Midget added. "Something only they can do. Like McDonalds, with their fuckin' arches."

"But how would you find guys who wanted to try

such a crazy thing?" Gina asked. "I mean, nobody's ever heard of this before."

"Oh, I could find 'em," Midget allowed. "You'd be surprised how many guys will try something just 'cause it's different. My cousin in Harrisburg used to work a girl who pretended she was retarded. She was actually very smart. She had a 'counting certificate from the JC. When she was with a guy she would only say things like, 'You got a candy stick I can lick, mister?' It was amazing how johns went for that. It's just too bad you didn't keep the tape, 'cause I think we could make us some real money with it."

It was typical of Midget to come up with a reason why he could not succeed.

They sat in silence until Sammi had a brainstorm: "I could make us a tape!"

"I don't know," Midget whined. "Don't take this wrong, but I just can't see you doin' it."

"Why the heck not? I used to be quite an actress. And I've been missin' the life, you know? I've been tryin' to figure out how I could get back in without screwin' up my home. If Gina told me what it said, I'll bet I could make a tape that was even better than the original."

Gina gave her a vote of confidence. She liked Sammi, and could relax around her. She hadn't heard any complaints about the older woman. Sammi's rep was that she had never tried to steal customers away when she'd been working, or pull any of the tricks that were so typical with the other girls. "I think you could," Gina agreed.

"Well, if we're gonna do it, we oughta do it before we change our mind," Midget declared. "If this ain't gonna be just more talk talk talk, then let's go up to my room and make a tape right now. I've got a fuckin' recorder, and some stuff to get us in the mood."

Gina had been talking hypothetically, but once Midget called her on it she was damned if she would back down. But then another idea made her hold back. "This ain't gonna be no freebie, Midget," she warned.

"What you talking about, girl!" he protested. "I never let pleasure get in the way of business, and this is business. Good business, I might add."

The three of them got up to go, with Gina leaving a five dollar bill. The working girls never ate much, but they appreciated the use of a warm place to sit down on their breaks.

Out on the street, Gina saw a parked green Ford Aerostar that looked familiar. She leaned down and looked in, and there sat The Professor, as taciturn and yet expectant as always. He had his lips drawn in, as if he was afraid some nefarious type was out to steal his false teeth. Next to him was the familiar paper bag, with its edges folded together twice. Despite his strange tastes he was a very neat man.

"Sorry, this guy's waiting for me," Gina told Sammi and Midget. "He pays extra good. We'll have to get together another time."

They both complained. Midget wanted her to blow off her john, saying they should make a tape while the idea was fresh in her mind. But Gina ignored them and got in the car.

"So, you can't stay away from your special treatment, eh?" she asked the driver, roughly pinching his cheek. "I think maybe I oughta give you a double dose. What d'you think?"

He could barely control his happiness.

Chapter 3

It was sweltering inside the TKD stamping plant the next day. Grime was dripping off the wall. It was humid as well as hot, and the ventilating system was behaving erratically once again. To top it off, the shaft on the main press had bent and it clanged thunderously as it spun through its cycle. Some of the workers gulped down handfuls of aspirin, while others were sneaking drinks in the rest rooms. The union rep was writing up a complaint in the lounge, but nobody was holding their breath.

As for the rumor that new money was coming in to revitalize the equipment, well, as far as the rank and file were concerned, it couldn't happen soon enough.

At lunch time the men sat listlessly in the cafeteria, too worn down by the hideous conditions to bother with their regular games of hearts or cribbage. As usual, Bob sat with Ray, Arnie with his pop-bottle glasses, and Dave, the regulars from his week-end poker parties. They were brown-baggers, but Bob always added one or two of the cafeteria's side dishes.

Tony sat across the room where he could observe them without being noticed. Ever since that poker game, he'd maintained his distance. They'd started their attack by mocking his nephew for his effeminate demeanor. Tony had defended him with his usual rejoinder: "He just acts that way because of his job in the flower shop.

When in Rome...."

Bob had been the worst. He'd kept repeating that queers weren't born that way, that somebody'd had to teach them. "Let's see, who's the pervert here?" Bob had pretended to muse, his eyes falling on Tony. The others had picked up on it, and now he felt that whenever they looked at him they heard an echo of Bob's booming voice.

The next day Bob had tried to make it up. His so-called apology, though, had been a thinly-disguised insult, and while shaking hands and smiling Tony had inwardly refused to forgive him. Tony had always gone out of his way to be nice to the boob, but the way Bob had pounced on him and then not let up was the worst form of treachery. He'd resolved to get even, no matter to what lengths he had to go. But actually coming up with a plan had not been easy.

The clock reached 12:30, provoking a general rustle as the 300 men in the large room headed back to their stations. Bob and Ray were on the line, and Arnie and Dave in electrical. Tony was part of a semi-independent section, running a gasket-maker in a kind of in-house out-sourcing. The position paid the same as the other jobs, but it had slipped through the cracks of the union contract so the fringes were not there. Tony tried to take the point of view that that gave him a higher status, which was only appropriate for a 1979 honors graduate from a two year program at the Ohio Technical Institute. Getting the boobs to agree had not gone well.

Work dragged on during the afternoon. Tony had several chances to get a glimpse of Bob. Whenever he looked, Bob was working away as though nothing had happened. It bothered Tony that Bob had not been more affected; he had hoped the experience would have left him too full of emotion to concentrate. Still, Bob's apparent equilibrium meant Tony could push forward with the second phase of his plan.

After work Bob and his friends headed for Spuds as usual, a tavern which many of the TKD employees frequented. Spuds sponsored an 8-ball league, but Tony thought it was a waste of energy. The few times he'd accepted an invitation to stop in, he preferred to nurse his drink and save his money. Why the flamboyant women who stopped in would fawn over someone who could hit a bank shot was beyond him.

Tony followed at a safe distance until he saw them park. Then he drove around for awhile. By the time he entered, Bob's group was enjoying life from a table near the corner. They had already finished off their first pitcher of beer.

Tony took a seat at the bar. At one point Ray noticed him and nudged Arnie, who nudged Bob in turn. None of them waved him over; his failure to have rolled with the punches of their kidding had driven a wedge into their formerly easy-going relationship. And Bob had given him the kiss of death the next day after his attempted apology had been thwarted, getting a laugh by remarking, "Maybe there is something to it then."

As the night wore on, Bob's friends gave up and went home one by one. But Bob stayed, switching from the pitcher to cans of Bud Lite. When Arnie, the last of them, stumbled out, Tony joined Bob at his table and offered to buy the next round.

"You're on," Bob accepted.

Once it arrived Tony began to act out the next stage of his plan. Speaking so low that Bob had to lean forward to hear, he said, "I had the damnedest thing happen to me a few nights ago. It was wild! I know I shouldn't tell anyone, but I can't just keep it to myself."

"What?" Bob asked, somewhat disinterested. He was watching the ace bowlers Linda and Lois, who had just come in. They had a reputation for ravaging men and then throwing them away, and Bob was wondering how to get them to take him on next. They had broken the arm of a guy from shipping in the heat of passion, and laughed in his face when he brought them his medical bills. Bob was drawn to the idea of rough sex: it was an exotic new domain for his mundane fantasies. Maybe he could show them how he'd become a pretty good spanker.

"If I tell you, you've got to promise not to ever breathe a word of this. I could get into real trouble, although I didn't do anything wrong. I mean, she just showed up at my place. Rang the bell. I opened the door, and, Jesus to Pete, there she was. Wrapped up like a birthday gift."

Bob's eyes widened. Now that he had Bob's attention, Tony feigned a reluctance to continue. "Maybe I better not say anything," he mumbled.

"Who showed up at your door? C'mon, you can trust me, I won't say anything."

"I never did find out her name," Tony began, lighting a cigarette. Then he proceeded to tell Bob a fabricated story, which was similar to Bob's own experience1— except Tony made his alleged visitor a large-breasted, early-30s woman who'd been restrained but fully dressed.

"The voice on the tape said, 'Please take my skirt and panties off. They're much too confining.' So I did. I mean, what the heck would you have done?"

Bob sat there with his mouth open, hardly able to move. Tony pretended not to notice how attentive he had become. "At first I suspected someone was playing a joke on me," Tony confided. "But this woman really enjoyed it. She did it just to have a gut-wrenching orgasm. It's what turned her on. It's so wild I still can't quite believe it."

It was too much for Bob. He had not wanted to say anything to Tony about his own experience, but this revelation made it impossible not to tell him. He blurted out that something similar had happened to him just the night before.

"You're kidding! Really?"

Once Bob started describing his experience, there was no holding back. A great gush of information spewed out, mixed with expressions of amazed appreciation. Noting the exaggerations, Tony fought back a smile. "It was unbelievable," Bob declared. "I had no choice, except to do what I was told."

"Maybe this is some new fad. Something that appeared in a women's magazine, or something."

"She said she just got here from California. Maybe this is what they're doing out West! That's a wild and crazy place."

"You may be right. According to Gordon Elliot, things that start out there have a good chance of spreading because they get all the media attention. Well if that's the case, I say, bring it on. Toledo is ready."

"You can say that again. Baby, bring it on!"

They sat there talking for awhile. Tony tailored his comments to try to make Bob think the phenomenon was rapidly expanding. Finally said he Tony had to get going. He pulled himself to his feet and leaned over for a well-rehearsed parting remark: "Let's hope she tells her friends, eh? I'd hate to think this was only a one-time shot. It's almost the perfect situation, eh? You don't have to wonder what she wants you to do next because she tells you in advance. What a relief."

On the way home Tony cruised past the boarded-up pharmacy where he had found Gina. She was standing there again, rocking back and forth to inaudible music and wearing a similarly provocative outfit. He went past her, made a U-turn, and came back and stopped.

She leaned down to see who it was, her face expressing a parody of excited surprise. But when she saw it was Tony she became more businesslike. "You again," she remarked. "What d'you want this time?"

"Just to talk," he said. He was disappointed that she did not share his feeling of having been coconspirators in something radical and exciting.

"I get a hundred bucks to chat," she shot back. That was another cardinal rule: once a price was established, there could never be a reduction.

"I just wanted to make sure you were okay. No delayed repercussions or anything. From the other night."

"I'm fine. Thanks for askin'. Now buzz off. You're scarin' away my customers. You look like a cop."

"I'm thinking about doing it again."

She drew back to study him for a moment. "Let me know when you make up your mind."

He fumbled for the right words. "Thing is, I want to do it to the same guy, but I want to use a different girl. I want him to think the world's finally listening."

"Hey, what's going on? Wasn't I good enough?"

"No, you were great! But ... it's like an extended practical joke. I want the guy to think this happens all the time."

"In your dreams!"

"In California, and that it's spreading here too. I, uh, I was wondering if you had a friend who you think would be willing to, uh, have the same experience."

Tony could see Gina's wheels begin to grind as she considered how to make this pay off. "Maybe," she finally hedged. "But it's gonna cost you."

"How much? I thought I was fair last time."

"She'll want $100. Then there's me."

"How about $50 as a referral fee?"

"Don't insult me. I'm better than she is."

"I'm not a rich man," he protested.

"That's not my fault, Jack. $200, and we've got a deal."

He enjoyed the negotiation, but eventually agreed. She opened his car door and jumped in, saying, "Let's go. She's workin' in the next block."

"Not tonight! I've got to get a new tape made first. I don't want it to be exactly the same. Pretty much the same, but a little different. How about tomorrow night?"

A light went on in Gina's head. "What d'you pay to have your tapes made, anyway? I've got a friend who's a really good actress. She has a very sexy voice. She used to be in the life, but she married a rich guy and quit. Except she's always comin' around to rub elbows. She could make you a hell of a tape."

"For how much?"

"$100. Shit is worth what you pay for it," she snapped.

"Jesus, you're milking me dry," Tony protested.

"And $100 for me."

He protested for a minute, but soon gave in; the overweight, middle-aged woman he'd recruited from a phone-sex service had gotten awfully suspicious, and he preferred not to have to deal with her again.

"Only thing is, I don't know if she'll be around tonight. You wanna go see?"

He agreed, so she directed him towards Wendell's. She had him park around the corner and wait.

According to Alice, the horse-faced waitress who all the working girls liked and trusted, Sammi had not yet come in. Gina asked if she could leave a message for her. "Just tell her to come find me. I gotta talk to her. You know my spot, don't you?"

"The fur store, right?"

"No, that's Rose's. I'm at the old pharmacy. Down the street from the furs."

"Oh yeh. I used to get a malted there every Saturday with my allowance when I was a kid," Alice reminisced, drifting back to a time when things sparkled.

Gina told Tony she had left a message for the actress, and made him drive her back to her stand. "You got a script or anything? That way she can practice it tonight, and we can get together tomorrow night, make the tape, and go drop the girl."

"Sounds like a plan," Tony told her, reaching in the glove compartment to get the script he had jotted down in ball-point during his breaks at work. "See you about 9:30 tomorrow?"

"Honey, you got yourself a date."

It was a slow night. Gina had two customers before midnight, and one after, a shy accountant-type who drove past her several times before working up the nerve to stop. She sensed he wanted to be reprimanded, or punished, and she was close: he wanted to masturbate himself while she watched, telling him she forbade him to go all the way and making him beg her to please, Please, PLEASE let him spurt.

As usual, she threw herself into her act. She prided herself on her professionalism, even though her degree of commitment frequently wore her out. It wasn't the sex that was so exhausting, but the pretense. One wrong intonation and it could all come crashing down. The sex wasn't even actually there; it was confined to her customers' fantasies. She usually stayed as dry as she had been with her stupid fuddy husband toward the end.

Parked behind the roller rink, she brought the accountant right to the edge and tried to keep him there as long as she could. She ordered him to slow down, making ripples of contradictory forces range across his brow. He was ordinarily a very capable person, but he did not know how to cope with her brash commands to hold himself in check. He became a pathetic little boy, afraid to go against the wishes of his leering disciplinarian.

There was something about his indecision she found a little arousing. As soon as she noticed the tingle, though, she shut it down. That was the first rule, which she never violated: allowing oneself to take any pleasure at all from the squalid imagination of the customers was the beginning of the end. "If you can't control yourself any better, I'm gonna give you the thrashing of your life," she barked. Her intensity was enough to send him over the edge. She laughed when he splattered the dash of his Aurora with his goopy cottage cheese.

He gave her an extra $20 when he dropped her off. "You better not even touch yourself 'till next time," she told him, smirking. "I'd know, and you wouldn't like what I'd do. When you comin' back?"

"Whenever you say," he whimpered, blinking away the hazy spots he was still seeing from the strain.

"You come and ask me if I have time for you, okay? I probably won't have, but I want you to ask. It wouldn't hurt for you to bring me some presents, you know."

"Like what?"

"Jesus, use your imagination!" She slammed the door and walked away, putting an extra swing in her stride until she heard him drive away.

The lack of business bothered her. It wasn't so much that she needed the money as that a successful encounter helped hold down the notion that she was not contributing anything to society. Just standing there by herself as the minutes raced past always brought out her inner judge, an amalgam of all the stern watchdogs who'd ever haunted her steps.

About 1:45 Sammi came by in her Viper, complaining that her husband had not gone to sleep until she gave him a double. "That guy came back!" Gina told her, climbing in. "The one from last night? He wants to do it again but with a different girl. He wants to make a slightly-different tape, too. I told him I knew an actress who'd do the voice."

"How much would I get?" Sammi asked. She was well-trained in the notion that pay conferred value.

"$100."

"That's all?"

"I figured we were gonna make a tape for ourselves

anyway, so we'll just give him a copy. I've got the guy's script!"

"Now you're talkin', girlfriend! Let's go wake up Midget and get to work!"

Sammi took off like a bat out of hell in her Viper, which she claimed was hotter than a Corvette. "The only thing girls get cars like this for is putting up with men with short cocks," she joked. "I saw a girl last week tooling around in a Mercedes. She looked so arrogant I wanted to holler, 'So you settled for Mr. Stumpy, eh?'"

Gina had never met Sammi's husband, but she had formed a picture of him: perhaps 50, capable, smart, rigid. Dignified on the surface but secretly addicted to kinky fantasies that he did not have the guts to act out. Marrying Sammi had been his compromise.

Midget lived above Preston's, a seedy liquor and magazine store on 4th Street. One night when he had come into Wendell's stoned out she had naturally probed for any secrets he might have. He told her how he had cut a hole in his floor between two joists so he could pull a throw rug back, lift out a section of wood, reach down and skid aside one of the acoustic panels in the store below's suspended ceiling, and climb down his home-made rope ladder to grab a beer and the latest Hustler. "The fuckin' clerk is convinced it's the fuckin' black kids who're stealin' him fuckin' blind," he had boasted. "Serve 'em right to get banned from the fuckin' store."

"Who would you put the blame on then?" Gina had

asked, bringing him up short.

Sammi and Gina parked on the side street and went up the wobbly back stairs. Midget responded to their knocks by asking who was there. After identifying themselves, they heard a toilet flush, followed by the sounds of a scramble. Finally Midget let them in.

The door opened into the kitchen. The room was a mess, and it stank. "Don't you ever clean?" Sammi complained. "Open the God-damned window!"

"I'd like to know how the fuckin' Welfare people expect anyone to live a decent life on their fuckin' meager checks," Midget replied, pushing the crust ends from an old pizza off his table and into the cardboard box that served as a waste basket. "Anyway, what's goin' on?"

Sammi did a little dip. "We got the script!" she announced, proudly waving it.

"Yes!" he said, jumping into a weird little celebratory dance of his own.

"You still got your recorder?" Gina asked.

That stopped him in mid-whoop. "Uh, I mean, Tink has it, but I'll go get it. Right now. He only lives two blocks away, okay? You stay here and rehearse. I'll be right back."

He ran out as they were disparaging him but turned around half way down the stairs. "Hey, Sammi, can I take your car?" he whined, sticking his head through the door.

"Just walk," she said. "If I gave you the key we wouldn't see you for a week!"

He grinned, proud that she credited him with knowing a ticket to a good time when he saw one. He was chomping at the bit for the chance to tell somebody about this repartee, albeit with a few changes. *If I let you screw me I wouldn't wanna stop for a week.*

Gina handed the script to her friend. While Sammi read it she went into the living room and poked around in the drawers of a dilapidated desk. She found a stack of unopened letters, all addressed to Mr. and Mrs. James Wainwrite II in Columbus and sent back marked, 'No longer at this address.' The returns had been to Jimmy Wainwrite III at a variety of addresses, the most recent being where he lived now. The postmarks went back 11 years.

"Hey, what's my motivation?" Sammi asked, coming into the living room holding the script in one hand and fiddling with her flamboyant tie with the other.

"I don't know. Same as always, I suppose. Havin' a good time and stayin' alive."

Fifteen minutes later footsteps on the stairs indicated Midget wasn't alone. Sure enough, Tink had insisted on tagging along, a gentle, moon-faced man whose hands were as disproportionally small as his girth was large.

"I'll be the engineer," he announced in a quivering bass voice. "I know a lot more about electronics than Midget."

At first the women rejected the idea, but Tink said he'd brought over some of his own equipment—including a special mike that would add to the sense of intimacy. He was a large, flabby man with unkempt eyebrows and not much hair on his head. Always polite, he had no self-confidence or ego. "What the hell," Sammi said, deciding the matter.

Tink began setting up in the living room as Sammi read through the script again.

"You've got to show how you gradually get worked up by increasing your breathing and stuff," Gina coached.

"I'm the one who was in Hello Dolly, remember?" she countered.

Finally they were all set. Pushing buttons, Tink cued Sammi to start. She was hesitant at the onset, which Gina thought was appropriate, but perked up as she got going. She finished in 35 minutes.

"It's supposed to last for 45," Gina told her.

"Jesus, Gina, that was just a trial run-through. Let's listen to it and see where to slow it down and what to add."

They played it back, with Sammi making marks in

the margins of the script: 'moan', or 'repeat last'. Midget and Tink quickly came under its pull, and sincerely praised Sammi's talent when it was done.

Midget excused himself to get some beer when they started the second take. Gina was tempted to follow him into his bedroom and pull up the rope ladder to trap him in the store below, but she let the impulse pass.

Gina had to admit she was surprised at Sammi's skill. She did an excellent job, infusing her role with just the right amount of emotion to make it seem real. Her initial fear gave way to mounting passion shortly past the mid-point.

Sitting cross-legged on the floor in front of his tape deck, Tink was transfixed. When Midget returned with four cans of Coors, he too sat in silent rapture until the tape was done.

"That's a take!" Gina exclaimed to her grinning friend. "Cut, and wrap."

Accepting a beer, Sammi proposed a toast: "Chase Manhattan bank, here we come!"

Chapter 4

The next night, Tony cruised past the boarded-up pharmacy, looking for Gina. He had been thinking about her all day. He was not nearly as nervous this time. Her business-like attitude excited him, and he imagined he had probably impressed her with the daring of his imagination.

It was only 8:15, but he had to listen to the tape, check out the girl Gina had found, get her dressed in the new burgundy spandex straight-jacket he'd prepared, and have her on Bob's doorstep no later than 10:30.

He made a U-turn, and parked down and across the street, where he could watch her turf. Not seeing her made him apprehensive. He hoped she wouldn't blow him off. He had never been any good at waiting, and now he began to fidget.

Worrying that a cop might stop to see why he was sitting there, he glanced at the back seat, where the new costume was packed in a box. He realized it was a mistake not to have put it in the trunk. If some cop wanted to see what was in it, what would he say? But to get out and put it in the trunk here was to risk being caught red-handed.

He decided to drive to a safer neighborhood, put the box in the trunk, and then drive back. He started the car but then turned it off, asking himself, 'What if she comes back and is picked up again while I'm gone?' Cars were slowing down. Every five or ten minutes a car crept past the curb with the driver peering into the shadows of the pharmacy's recessed entry.

At 8:55 Tony's passenger door opened and a radiant Gina got in. He was delighted to see her, but he couldn't help complaining: "Where've you been? I've been waiting here for almost an hour!" It was a way of asserting a proprietary interest.

"Listen, idiot, you said 9:30. Remember?" she shot back.

Chastened, he asked her if she had made the tape.

She held it up, but pulled it back when he grabbed for it. "Have you got my money?"

He reached in his pocket and showed her a fan of bills, but wanted to listen to the tape before paying her. "That's not the way it works," she countered. She was adamant, so he gave her the money. "That's a good boy," she cooed, smiling and handing him the cassette.

He put the tape in a player from the glove compartment and turned it on.

"It runs 45 minutes," Gina said. "I ain't got all day. Skip around, so you get the idea."

He obeyed, listening to the opening, two snatches in the middle, and the grand finale. She was delighted to see a smile form on his lips as Sammi spun her spell.

"It's great," Tony told her, overly sincere. "Your friend really has a talent for this."

He ran the tape back to the beginning. "Let's get your friend," he said, starting the car.

They drove to the fur store, where Rose got in the back seat. Gina handed her the $100 they had agreed on earlier in the evening. Rose had been relieved; she was coming down with something that was sapping her strength, and the routine with the tape promised to be easier on her than an unrehearsed encounter. And she needed more money than ever now, what with Angel's teeth not coming in straight.

Honestly, sometimes she wished she knew where the father had gone.

"That's your costume in the box," Tony said, looking at her in his rear view mirror. She had a matter-of-fact charm that made him stare.

"You sure it's my size?" Rose teased, picking up on his fascination. She automatically fanned his interest by flaring her nostrils and injecting a sensual rhythm in her speech.

"One size fits all," Tony replied.

His laugh caught in his throat, which Rose took as a victory. "Are you sure?" she teased. "I'm a little bounteous in places."

Tony headed for Vinewood on the back streets. Rose

pulled off her halter-top and Miracle Bra, shaking herself more than was necessary when she saw she still had Tony's attention. Smiling, she examined the spandex suit. "Oh, look, it's got peek holes for my titties," she said, shaking them again.

"You know what to do?" Tony asked her.

"Act excited and let some dude spank me and poke me while the tape gives him instructions," she answered. "It'll be a vacation."

"I wanna ride along," Gina said. Tony hadn't anticipated this but had no objections. He liked her quick mind and open point of view.

They parked down from Bob's bungalow. Somebody had cut down a chestnut tree across the street and sawed up the trunk and branches into firewood, which was stacked between the sidewalk and curb. Killing the engine, he told the women they would wait ten minutes, just to make sure.

"Time's money," Gina said.

"Rushing into something gets you in trouble," Tony countered. "That's where you lose money."

"What're you, a fuckin' philosopher?" Rose badgered, smiling provocatively at his eyes in the mirror.

Tony and Gina helped Rose slither out of her short skirt and into her costume. "I'm getting hot already just wearing this," she teased, looking into Tony's eyes penetratingly enough to make him blush. To calm himself he lit a cigarette, and then a second for Gina, who shared puffs with her friend. The street was quiet. The lemonade stand still sat forlornly while its owners were away. It had been another dry day, and all traces of the showers of two days before had disappeared.

When he finished his cigarette Tony declared it was time. He came around to the passenger side and opened the back door. She kept her eyes on him as he put the hollow plastic ball in Rose's mouth and applied another set of the bright, sensuous lips he'd used with Gina. Pulling her hands across her belly, he locked the sleeves together behind her back—producing a brief moan. A tall woman, her high heels put her at his level as she leaned into him for stability. Her eyes gave her a wild, devil-may-care independence.

He checked his pocket for the blindfold and then strapped the small tape player around her neck. He removed a new placard from the trunk. Gina rolled her window down, saying, "Let's see, let me see!" He held it there long enough for her to read:

Hi! From what I hear, I'll bet you're the perfect man for me. If you're willing to see if I'm right, please bring me inside, remove my blindfold, and push the 'play' button. I promise to make you as happy as this will make me, which I know will be very very happy. Thank you very much.

"It's different," Gina commented, thinking she could've done better.

Tony mumbled, grabbed the duffel and placard, and helped Rose down the street to Bob's modest home. Once he'd positioned her properly, he put the blindfold over her eyes, rang the bell, and darted into the hedge.

The door opened. Tony could hear Bob remark, "Well well, what the hell have we here?"

Tony crouched lower as Bob walked past Rose out to the street, dangling a long-neck. Bob looked both ways, saw nothing suspicious, and returned. Tony heard shuffling, and then the door closed. When he peeked around the corner Rose had disappeared inside.

He loped back to his car. "Did he see you?" he asked Gina.

"Naw, I ducked down. So now what?"

"Now we wait."

She was silent for awhile but then started asking questions. Exactly what was he doing? Why? What did he plan to do next? He explained that this was personal, but that only made her ask her questions again in slightly different phrasings.

"Look, I'll tell you, okay?" he finally said. "The guy in there started saying I was ... a pervert or something. A sicko. It began as a joke, but then he latched onto it and wouldn't let it drop. He got my friends thinkin' that maybe there was something to it."

"So?"

"So, he's always so self-righteous, as if he would never do anything out of the ordinary. I started thinkin', he just hasn't had the chance. I kept thinking about it, and thinking about it, and finally I decided to give him one."

"He's right, you are weird," Gina told him.

He drew back, wrinkling his brow.

"Relax," she said. "I like that. All my friends have a screw loose, one place or another. You're my kind of dude."

He glanced at her, and then looked back straight ahead. "Uh, maybe there's a better way to pass the time than just sitting," he said, swallowing audibly and glancing at her again.

"Forget it! That's business, which I never mix with pleasure. Right now I'm enjoying just talking, so let's leave it at that."

Hurt, he lit another cigarette, and stared out the front window.

"What're you gonna do next?" Gina asked, grabbing his cigarette and taking a toke.

"I don't think I should say," he pouted.

"C'mon, you've gone this far. Tell me."

He looked at her, his expression changing to that of a naughty boy being forced to confess some terrible sin of which he was secretly proud.

"Spit it out," Gina ordered. "Or don't you trust me?"

"Well, I was thinking ... maybe I'd grab someone, you know, off the street, a woman who wasn't in on it. I'll get her trussed up in a costume and bring her over here. He'll take her inside, thinking she's just another kinky number, but when he frees her afterwards she'll throw a fit and call the cops, and then everyone will see he's a hell of a lot sicker than I ever was."

"Jesus," Gina whispered. "You really are sick."

"What? I just want to show him I'm not someone to mess with. What's the big deal?"

She looked at him sternly at first but turned appreciate before responding. "I suppose you'll try to grab someone he knows," she finally said. "His friend's wife, or his overweight, religious cousin who sings in the church choir out in Pigsville. With a wig and the right make-up he'd never recognize her until the tape was done and he set her free."

Once he realized she wouldn't condemn him he began to breathe more easily, and the helpless, slightly embarrassed look that had seized his face drained away. "I hadn't thought that far ahead, but that's a good idea," he said.

"I used to do a deal in Atlanta where I'd say to a guy afterwards, 'If you can get it up again, and you got another fifty bucks, I'll go upstairs and send my friend down. You'll like her, she's a lot tighter than me.' See, guys never pay the same woman to do it twice. They think they got it comin' for all the pleasure they'd given. So I'd go upstairs, put on different lingerie and a wig, and come back and do the guy a second time."

"Really?"

"Guys are such jerks. They believe whatever you tell 'em when they're in that state. Most of 'em would say I was much better than my friend. Jesus, you can feed them almost anything when they're jacked up and they'll repeat it back to you like they got it from the Bible."

"You're an awfully smart person to, uh, be leading this kind of life. How come?"

"Why do you think? I'm making up for two years of a stupid boring marriage."

He added, accepting the bullshit she had randomly thrown out. The way he responded made her think more fondly of him, as if he were like a kindred spirit, or the older brother she'd never had. He noticed her look but before he could think of what to do there was movement at Bob's house: the door opened, and Bob peeked out. "Holy shit, it's only been six or seven minutes," Tony exclaimed. "Something's wrong."

A moment later Bob led the still-blindfolded Rose outside and helped her into his Pontiac, which was parked in the drive. After sitting her in the passenger seat he scurried back for the placard, which had been left leaning against the post supporting the little plastic roof over the stoop, and then got in the driver's side and pulled into the street. "What the hell! We've got to do something!" Gina screamed. "I got her into this, so I'm responsible. This is fucked!"

Tony started his car and drove after Bob. Gina wanted him to pull Bob over, but he hung back, telling her that they should see what he was doing before they intervened.

"Whatever it is, it can't be good! Who knows what that jerk is thinking. He could be taking her out to the boonies to whack her! We've got to stop him!"

"Listen, if he tries anything I'll ram him," Tony promised.

Suddenly Gina was overcome with hatred of Tony for his over-cautiousness. A little man, leading a little life. When he glanced at her he could see how she felt, but he was unable to bring himself to do more than follow.

Bob was heading east. When a sign announced they had entered Shakerton Village, Tony realized what was going on. "He's takin' her to his buddy Ray's house," he announced.

"He's an asshole. He deserves whatever you do to him."

Luckily, Tony was right. They followed Bob to where he stopped down the street from Ray's house, and parked 200' behind him. Bob sat there for a minute, and then came around to get Rose out of the car. Carrying the placard in one hand, he helped her navigate falteringly up to Ray's house, and then positioned her in front of the door.

"We gotta do somethin'," Gina urged.

"What?"

"I sure as hell don't know, but I can tell you this: when people stop followin' the plan, the deep shit comes along."

Ray opened the door, found Rose, and spending after a moment to comprehend his good fortune took her by the arm and helped her inside. Chuckling, Bob came back to his car.

"We could call the cops," Tony suggested.

"Fuck, that would be worse! They'd bust everybody. You have to go in there and get her! This is your deal, so you have to make it right!"

"Jesus, let me think!" He was silent for a minute and then had an idea: "We could phone Ray. You could talk to him and say you wanted to warn him that the cops got a tip and are on the way so he better let your sister go right away."

"What about that idiot just parked there?" Gina asked. "If the guy inside lets Rose go, this goofball will just grab her again."

Tony's brow was being tied into knots. "You better call the cops first. Tell them you live across the street, and some weirdo who's been watching your kids is sitting outside jacking off in his car. Then call Ray."

Tony backed to the corner with his lights off, and then sped toward a convenience store a few blocks away. "No way!" she protested. "I'll call the guy who's got Rose, but I ain't talkin' to no cops. It's against my philosophy."

Tony agreed. He made the first call, saying he was worried about a guy who was casing his neighbor's house and giving Ray's address. He added that the guy looked like a pervert who was hoping one of the children would come out in the yard. Then Tony dialed Ray's number and Gina whispered into the receiver, saying, "The cops are comin', buddy. You don't deserve to go to jail just for havin' a little fun, so you better let that woman leave now."

By the time they got back to Ray's a squad car had already pulled in front of Bob and was sitting there with its lights flashing while the officers listened to him try to explain what he was doing there. Past him, Rose was walking down the street; she'd had enough presence of mind to have grabbed the placard. Tony and Gina let her turn the corner before picking her up.

"What the hell was that all about?" she demanded, angry.

"I'm terribly sorry, it wasn't part of the plan," Tony

apologized.

"Uh huh. All I know is I get double when shit starts goin' wrong," Rose insisted. "You're just lucky as hell that I'm willing to let it go at that, mister. You're just lucky as hell."

Feeling that this was an honest assessment, he didn't quibble, and steadied his hands enough to count out another $100. Rose took the bills with the attitude that this wasn't nearly enough.

"Don't forget about me," Gina chirped, suddenly as angry as her friend. "My fee's double as well."

Chastised, Tony kept counting.

Chapter 5

The women arrived at Wendell's at a little after 1:00 a.m., where they had agreed to meet Sammi. The experience of overcoming the way things had gone bad had given them an extra dollop of self-confidence. Their cockiness had attracted more customers than usual, and by the time they went to the restaurant they felt they were done working for the night.

Sammi was already there; they saw her Viper across the street. As soon as they walked through the door she got up from the table of women she'd been sitting with and led Rose and Gina to a booth at the back. "Well?" she asked as they sat down. "How'd it go?"

Despite Sammi's anxiousness, Gina waited to reply until Alice had taken their orders: steak and eggs for Rose, eggs over easy for Gina, both with large coffees. "Not as planned," she began, struggling to look morose for a minute before giving up and adding brightly, "Better than planned!"

"That was one hell of a tape," Rose said. "You're really talented!" Gina had played it for her after her escape.

"Except the dufus decided it was so good he couldn't keep it all to himself," Gina continued. The two of them took turns telling the story, interrupting each other back and forth to add details the other forgot. To cap it off,

Gina gave Sammi the $100 she had collected from Tony for making the tape.

"Jesus Christ," Sammi exclaimed, "biz money again. I'd sworn off it, but now I'm startin' to fuckin' tingle all over again. It feels good!"

She left it sitting on the counter, as if it were a trophy, or a charm that would continue to radiate good luck. "So, the doodlehead really liked it, huh?" she asked.

"Loved it," Gina said. "You're better than Jane Fonda."

"Hey, know what? We oughta have a little party to celebrate!" Rose gushed.

Sammi thought it would be a good idea, and furthered the plan by suggesting they get some beer and some coke and go over to Midget's. She offered to kick in $50.

Gina matched her, leaving Rose no choice but to do the same. It upset her for a moment. She'd been thinking that if she put her $200 into the fund for her daughter's braces, it would put her past the half-way mark. But if she had only learned one thing, it was that you had to be flexible. So after a brief hesitation she kicked in her share as well.

The three women squeezed into the Viper and zipped over to 8th Street, where a new connection was manning the corner. This dealer was surprisingly dependable and could speak decent English; either trait should have tipped off his customers that he was the point man for a sting. But since he had good stuff, nobody gave it a second thought.

The narcs who were parked across the street considered busting the three women. That would give them the option, one of them remarked, of "poking the broads and letting 'em walk, or takin' 'em down and keepin' their wheels." But the other reminded him that the real purpose of the operation was to catch Eddie Garafolo.

"Eddie's got a hard nose. He's bound to come by here to score, sooner or later."

"You think he'll roll over on his old man?"

"Maybe not. But we can approach Louie, tell him to give us something or his kid goes down. There are any number of plays we can put on."

"He'll know it's entrapment, man."

"Still, at least we'll open up a dialogue, right?"

They agreed, and reluctantly let the transaction go down, although for the next half hour they regaled each other with lascivious stories of what might have been. Two guys and three women presented several interesting possibilities.

The girls parked on the side street, and surprised Midget when they started up the steps. He was doing something outside, between his building and the apartment house next door, and almost jumped out of his skin when he saw them.

"Shhh!" he said when they all started talking. He leaned a shovel against his building and joined them on the stairs, carrying some hand tools. Once they were inside his apartment, he explained that he had just tapped into the cable supplying the dwelling next door.

"Don't they check their lines periodically to make sure that don't happen?" Rose asked.

"All I know is, that's the way it was when I moved in," Midget protested, grinning at the audacity of his lie. "I thought it was included for the rent."

"How much d'you pay, anyway?"

"I don't know, Welfare takes care of it direct."

"They don't trust you," Gina teased.

"It's just that they're all screwed up. Nobody who works there knows their ass from a hole in the ground. I've been telling them, they should put me in charge. Right?"

"Hey, I got some coke," Sammi told him.

Midget's eyes lit up, and the lid he had injured in a tussle with a girl several years back began its butterfly pirouettes.

"Maybe we should invite Tink," Rose suggested.

"What you got in mind?" Midget wondered, looking

both suspicious and hopeful.

"Getting down. Celebrating our success with the tape," Sammi put in. "Here," she added, handing Midget the final $50 from their pool. "Why don't you go get Tink. Buy a case of beer, and then you and him split what's left. The girls did well."

The money instantly disappeared into his pocket. He turned on the TV for them to watch while he went to get Tink, but the screen only produced fluctuating static. "Shit! Needs a little adjustment," he said, clicking it back off and leaving.

"You're a fuckin' genius all right," Gina yelled after him.

The women sat down at the kitchen table, determined to wait, but all they could think about was the coke. After a few minutes its shimmering promise became too strong to resist. Sammi got out the folded-over paper; Rose dug in her purse for her razor knife; and Gina washed and dried one of the plates piled in the sink. They made a highly efficient team.

"We're thinkin' of you, guys," Rose apologized to the air as she took her turn.

Gina's hit made her remember the letters in Midget's desk. She jumped up and went into the other room, where she did a double-take at finding an old exercise bike, a children's cart, and a can of gas with a barbecue grill. "What's this?"

Rose answered. "Didn't I tell you? Midget's a thief."

Shaking her head, Gina grabbed a letter and returned to the kitchen. Using Rose's knife, she slit it open and began to read the four-year-old message out loud: "Dear Mom and Dad. Things are going well. My boss has been hinting about a promotion. It will mean more responsibility. Which I can handle. Maybe another hundred dollars a week. You remember me mentioning Molly. If this goes through ...."

She stopped, and glanced around, almost embarrassed.

"The poor little mouse," Rose said, breaking the impasse.

"You know what we oughta do?" Sammi inquired. "We should get some guy to make us a tape of all Midget's phony letters, and then we oughta tie him up and gag him and drop him at his parents' door with it playin', eh?"

They all laughed, although it didn't really make any sense. "Pathetic little fucker!" Gina tenderly inveighed. "His parents are probably long dead. If he ever had any. He might've been hatched." There was a brief, somber moment, and then they started laughing uproariously again.

"Or, let's find him a Molly," Rose said. "We could have a girl read Midget's letters, and make him believe they were about to come true. The Molly he dreamed up comes to life. That's just like some fuckin' fairy tale, ain't it?"

"Puss 'n boots," Sammi offered.

Shaking her head, with giggles erupting periodically, Gina stuck the letter back in the envelope and put it back in the drawer. Then it was her turn for another hit. "Everybody's got a right to their dreams," she declared, accepting the rolled-up bill from Rose.

"No matter how fuckin' sorry they are," Sammi seconded.

The excitement of the two men showed in the way they scurried up the stairs. Tink had been sound asleep. He had to work the next morning as a part-timer at Radio Shack, but he said he could do what the job required even if he were half zonked.

As soon as he entered Midget turned off the overheads and brought in his special 'coke lamp,' whose blue light would let them pick out any impurities and remove them with a tweezers. "It cost two hundred bucks," he claimed.

"I can't imagine you spending two hundred dollars for a lamp," Gina said.

"I never said I paid for it."

"Bull shit," Sammi pronounced. "I've got the same blue bulb in my aquarium."

Everyone focused on Tink when Sammi passed him the plate, which made him blush. Struggling to control his breathing, he vacuumed up both the lines Sammi had made for him and those she'd arranged for Midget, who complained loudly, "Hey, dimwit! You done mine too!"

Sammi took the plate back and chopped a fresh clump for Midget. It was apparent to everyone that she was in charge of dispensation.

"I don't feel nothin'," Tink complained. "Is this stuff any good? Maybe you got ripped off. What'd this cost? Is it okay to put it on a plate—or might there be some ionic exchange? Maybe we should put in the fridge for awhile, or mix it with magnesium. Hey, I know where we can grab an isomer of tungsten so if you ever need any just give me a call."

"Not feeling anything is the first sign you're getting off," Gina teased.

"And the second sign is you can't stop blabbering," Rose added.

Tink started to sneeze. "Turn your head!" Sammi ordered, reaching to cover the plate. It turned out to be a false alarm.

Midget took a hit and then opened everyone a Coors. Laughing, Rose told her story again: the tape starting, the dufus getting into it, and then the fathead deciding to share the wealth. "She had to call the cops!" Sammi exclaimed.

"Not me!" Gina insisted. "I called the second dufus! Told him he was about to go down. Our fuck-head patron called the cops! Mr. Out for Revenge."

They joked back and forth, drinking beer and snorting coke. During a temporary lull someone asked what was next.

That reigned in the celebration. Gina explained how the guy who had gotten her into this had done it as an extended practical joke, but now that the cops were involved she thought he was unlikely to continue.

"We don't need him!" Midget announced. "We got all we need. We got two girls, an actress, a technical genius" —Tink beamed at the allusion— "and me. A business mastermind. What more do we need?"

"Someone with an actual brain," Rose joked.

"I'm serious! I'll bet there's lots of ways we can score with this," Midget persisted.

"Oh yeah? Name one," Sammi challenged.

"Well, listen, this phenomenon came from California, right? It's big out there, you said."

"I made that up! You're the dufus."

"Still. That means it'll be gettin' bigger here. Not as big as out there, probably, because we never quite measure up. We're too conservative. Sometimes I think I should move to L.A.."

"What's your point?" Gina demanded.

"Yeah, what's your point?" Tink chimed in.

"Just this. It's gonna get bigger here than it is now. We're in the middle of this. We could be the first participants in Ohio. There's gotta be a way we can make our position and experience pay off."

"Like how?" Rose wanted to know.

Gina shook her head, amazed at how her friends could make real-life plans based on a fictional situation.

But Midget was on a roll. "I don't know," he whined. "Let me think. We know about the costume, right? One of you women's got to have a sewing machine."

"Duh, no."

"Well, someone must. Maybe Angie. She looks like she makes her own clothes. So we can make costumes, right? And we can make tapes. Tink copied the one we already made."

"You do?" Sammi asked.

Tink blushed, and then finished off his beer. Belching, he opened another and eyed the remaining coke. In his eyes it had become an interesting new life form.

"We could make more copies off that one. Or, we could modify the script, and make others. Right? The sky's the limit."

"Sure, but what do we do with 'em?"

"We turn 'em into money. There's any number of ways," Midget boasted.

"For example?" Sammi persisted.

"Well, for example, we, uh, offer a service. We put ads in some of the papers, you know, in the Meet People section. We, uh, we offer to, uh, send a girl over to anyone interested in the new California tape craze, okay?"

"Is that what they call it? There's gotta be a better name for it than that," Sammi declared.

"Wonder what they call it in California?" Rose asked.

"Girls on Tape?" Tink guessed.

"Girls Following the Script?" Gina suggested, playing along. "Or maybe, Girls with Naughty Chaperons. On Tape. Or, Girls who Come Complete with Instructions."

Rose moaned at the clankiness of the suggestions.

"We've got to have more than one tape. There has to be variations," Sammi joked.

"How about one where there's more spanking," Midget asked. "Or one where the girl spanks the guy she visits. I'll bet you anything that'd be a big hit!"

"Nobody likes that," Rose said.

"Oh yeah?" Midget challenged. "That just shows how much you know! For your information, there's three different magazines devoted to the spanking arts."

"Well I guess we know what you like," Sammi replied. He protested, but gave himself away by turning red.

"I think we ought to give Midget a good spanking right now," Gina purred, glancing around for support. "Pull his pants down and really tan his fanny. Not stop until he agrees to become a good lap dog."

"You know what we need? A sequence of tapes," Sammi said. "One tape with just foreplay...."

"What the hell is foreplay?" Gina interrupted. "Isn't that something they used to do before the French Revolution?"

Laughing, Rose nodded wildly. "I heard about that once."

"....and then a tape of getting missionary, and then tapes for other positions. The Spread Eagle. The Montana Buckaroo. The Bird on a Wire. People could subscribe, and work their way up the series. We could send 'em a new girl once a week."

"You could even have a wedding tape," Tink volunteered.

"Wedding?" Sammi asked.

"Sure!" Rose piped up, liking the idea. "Lots of guys have that fantasy, and would get off from acting it out. Or so I'm told!"

"Dearly beloved...." Sammi intoned in a mock baritone. "Pull down your fuckin' pants!"

"Then we'd have to have a divorce tape, too!" Gina added. "Dear John. This is your one last time and then you'll never see me again. So make the best of it."

Sammi parceled out the last of their hundred-dollar bag. It was past 3:00 a.m.. Despite the coke, Tink was having a hard time staying awake.

"Hey, what would happen if we sent a girl to some dude's house, and when the door opened, he was standing there with a tape player of his own hung around his neck?" Gina asked. "It could happen!"

"If some guy gets used to only doin' it with a girl wearing a tape, imagine, he might ask his wife to wear one or else he won't be able to get it up!" Rose threw out. "Lots of guys make their wives try the tricks we teach 'em, you know. It never works, though, because they don't try hard enough. Straights never realize how much work it takes to have a good time. All that dead meat takes time and energy to animate."

"It ain't that," Sammi declared disconsolately. "It's that they let themselves get sucked into the action. They forget they're just puttin' on a fuckin' show."

They finished off the coke, and stood up to go. They

felt a little dizzy, but good, happy to have had their little party. Especially Tink, who was aglow and felt like he was floating in the air. To regain his self-control he began reciting the periodic table to himself but broke out in a sweat when he could not remember what came after molybdenum.

A lot of ideas had been thrown out, as was usual for coke-powered evenings. Midget kept saying they should get together soon to work out the details of their plan. Gina agreed, but only to be polite. She had learned that evenings like this were ends in themselves, and if one tried to recapture the spirit, it never turned out as well as one hoped.

Chapter 6

After Gina left the High-Hat Motel on Woodward Avenue back in Detroit nine months earlier, events had not unfolded as she had anticipated. She'd rushed past Gus Litwak, her husband, leaving him staring at the seeping bag of fat that had been Vincent Vandelay. All she remembered was the strangely bewildered expression on the normally-complacent man's face.

As she headed south, a number of possibilities of what might follow suggested themselves. Gus might have been so upset by having found his wife with the Assistant Chief of Police that he would simply sit there until the shocked Latino cleaning girl screamed, prompting the manager to call the cops. Or, Gus might become so unhinged by having killed Vandelay that he would load up again and eat his gun, rather than subjecting himself to the inevitable, painful, demeaning consequences. Or maybe Gus would ditch the gun and then wait to see what happened, hoping Vandelay had told somebody who he had intended to meet so that the full attention of the police would be focused on his runaway wife.

The latter seemed most likely, and that was the one with which Gina had been living. Thinking 'they' were after her had made her cautious. Several times she had given up a good thing and moved on because she had sensed that trouble was fast approaching; she was always reading the signs. Other girls would stand tough, taking the hit and just bailing themselves out. But Gina never took the chance of having her past catch up. She had heard Gus's stories about what could do when he made up his mind. She would never forget the cold hatred in his eyes when he aimed his gun at her, and his rage at himself for not being able to pull the trigger. She wasn't the kind of fool to give him a second chance.

Actually, she didn't have it quite right. The police weren't looking for her. As far as they were concerned, Vandelay had simply disappeared. Gus had been thorough. He had wrapped Vandelay's ungainly body in the shower curtain, stuffed it in his trunk, and dropped it in 20' of Lake St. Claire sludge from a borrowed boat, with a forty-pound concrete block strapped to his chest. Then he had made an anonymous call to a thief he knew: "there's a bird's-egg-blue Caddy in the High Hat Motel lot with the keys in it, and the owner won't be back 'till tomorrow." It had been stripped down and left in front of one of Detroit's many burned-out buildings before the sun came up the next day.

Vandelay's disappearance prompted much finger-pointing. There was talk about missing pension funds. No body had ever turned up, and their guess was that the rumors were true: the Assistant Chief had been living a double life, and finally his alter ego had taken control and he'd gone off with whatever he had been able to appropriate from the treasury to give himself over to his lucky evil self. He had become a kind of folk hero to the men on the force: he was the one who screwed the system and got away.

Gus's friends were solicitous about his wife, particularly Richard Spezio. "Even though she ran off, you were lucky to have had her while you did," he sympathized. "She always struck me as being a fine woman."

"I'll get over it," Gus had replied, biting his lip to keep up the charade of not knowing. "It ain't the first time it happened with a God-damned broad."

"That's the spirit, old buddy," Lieutenant Spezio told him, slapping him on the back. "Plenty more out there, eh? Remind me to take you to Millie's sometime. They have two Chinese sisters there who are amazingly inventive. Plus I get a fuckin' discount."

But Gus had discreetly investigated. He learned much about his wife's lifestyle, her affairs and her money. He made inquiries all over the country and checked out the reports. Most of them were ridiculously off-base but he believed a few had been right on. One time he flew to Cincinnati, thinking he would catch her, but she had pulled out just the day before.

He heard she showed up in Columbus. Before he decided what to do, his contact called back to say she had already left. Her inability to be content in any one place gave Gus a little pleasure, but that paled in comparison to the exhilaration he felt when he penciled the sightings of her on a map and drew a line through these points. It revealed that she was heading home. The thought of how he would react if he saw her again, and how he might finally get his revenge, gave him a deep sense of the world being manageable. Anticipating the various forms their meeting might take was one of his two strongest passions.

He was still on the police force, stuck at detective, feeling that people above him would never allow him to rise any farther. Spezio and his friends. But that was okay; he had recently found himself a few safe scams to provide the income to which he was, by all rights, entitled. He was putting money aside, and keeping his eyes open for a chance to make a serious score.

He was dating Margaret Stormhauser, a widow living in Gibraltar, a nautically-oriented suburb to the south. She was intelligent, urbane, and treated him as though his droll outlook implied a great hidden wisdom. She was a little over-weight, but he wasn't interested in a physical relationship so that did not matter. On her part she had learned what to expect out of life, and guarded herself against making any undue demands.

They went out every Saturday, trying restaurants recommended by the Free Press and then taking in a show. Sometimes they went to the Detroit Institute of Art on Sunday afternoon, where she would discreetly drop a hint or two about what he was seeing while pretending not to understand it herself.

She kissed him on the cheek when he favorably compared her to a Modigliani.

She was attentive to his whims, and frequently complimented him, but not so often as to make him suspect her sincerity. They would conclude the evening by watching a rented video and drinking a bottle of California wine, and critique them on the phone early the following week. They had a comfortable relationship, although she continued to be privately disappointed at his lack of sexual needs.

It was not that he was preoccupied with trying to find his wife. He rarely thought about her—usually only when a fresh lead developed. His daily attention was consumed by his second passion: tripping up the traitor Spezio. He blamed him for two things: seducing his wife; and then not being man enough to keep her under control. He had no idea exactly how she had been passed to Vandelay, but he was sure Spezio had been behind it. What made it worse was that he believed Spezio had used his wife to curry favor, which had led to promotions for Spezio that he should have been given instead. He was by far and away the better man.

Gus told Margaret he could rarely see her during the week because he was on call for his job. "Just seven more years," she remarked, alluding to the freedom he would have once he had made his pension. But the truth was, he was always on call for his own personal project: keeping tabs on Spezio, waiting for a chance to bring him down.

Spezio assumed Gus didn't know about his relationship with Sherri. As far as he was concerned, it was over and done with, as forgotten as any of his many other comparable affairs. She had been a hot little number, but so what? He was too busy with his current after-work operation to have any time to reminisce.

Spezio and his team had branched out. They were perpetuating a gang war between two crack-dealing families, who they called the Bucks and the Jolts. They were good at playing both sides against the other. Spezio did the talking. After his team, operating on information from the Bucks, hit a Jolts' outpost, taking whatever drugs and cash could be found, Spezio would commiserate with the Jolts' leader: "If you want, we can hit 'em back for you. It's better for you to keep your hands clean in case anything ever comes out. Won't those fucks ever learn? They must be crazy. Just tell me where they've set up."

Spezio's team, acting with professional efficiency, hit one or the other of the gangs every three weeks. Once they sold the dope their take averaged over a hundred grand. In the six months they had been doing this, they had almost reached $1,000,000. Spezio kept the booty in a safe place, but all five men had an equal share.

His avowed goal was for them to have $1,000,000 each. To reach it as quickly as possible Spezio kept an eye out for the possibility of larger scores. His secret dream was to concoct a scheme in which he could grab all the assets of both gangs and then put the members away. Salve his conscience. The leaders and anyone whom they had told about Spezio's involvement would have to be dealt with more severely. That would only be fitting, he thought, because those who became the leaders were only able to do so by developing a complete indifference to the value of life. The world would be better off without them.

What Spezio wanted for his efforts was millions of dollars and a special commendation, suitable for framing on the houseboat he planned to live on in the Caribbean. He would anchor half-way between the hungry young whores in one of the third-world port towns and the pristine blue-green waters he frequently fished in his imagination. He could not count the times he had landed a record marlin in his imagination. Sometimes he spent an entire stake-out picturing himself on this boat, bobbing slowly up and down, watching his bait and listening to a report on the upswing of his portfolio by short wave as a girl who could have graced the pages of Chocolate Beauties adjusted the itchy strap of her thong bikini, continuing to smile.

Maybe he'd write a best-seller.

Once they reached their goal, their plan was to chuck it in. After all, there was a certain degree of danger. In the meantime, he believed that all they had to do was guard against over-confidence and let the rewards continue to accumulate. The only possible problem was that somebody would figure it out, maybe one of the police department's Internal Affairs creeps. Maybe Gus Litwak, who had become a straight-arrow jerk.

"Does it seem to you he's asking too many questions about where we go and what we do?" Spezio asked Carpenter, the hulking senior member of the team.

Carpenter had never been fond of Litwak. He didn't know why, but when Spezio said he was unctuous—and then explained what it meant: a phony moralist; a hypocrite—it sounded right. From then on, Litwak's image always called the word to mind. "He's an unctuous fuck," Carpenter would volunteer, looking at his boss for approval.

"We better keep an eye on him," Spezio decided. They were drinking shots at Mickey's on Livernois in the middle of another boring shift, half watching two middle-aged women stretch to take their shots on the old-fashioned snooker table in the rear and then giggle and bat their eyes when they missed. Crows trolling for a worm.

"He ain't no threat," another member threw out. This young blond-haired cop from Illinois was the newest part of the team. An extreme racist, he was involved in their scam for the sport as much as anything. Spezio did not like him or trust him, but pretended to while subtly grooming Carpenter to hate Litwak in case something would have to be done.

"He's too busy trying to find his wife," the recruit added, filling the silence.

Spezio had not realized this.

"Oh yeah. He's got a network out there, lookin'. He asked me to give him some names on Chicago vice in case she went that way. He said he almost caught up to her twice. It's only a matter of time," he confidently pronounced.

Suddenly Spezio choked on worry, thinking 'if he gets her, she'll spill the beans about her and me for sure!'

"I bet you're right about Gus becoming a danger to us," Spezio said to Carpenter, making it seem that the idea had come from him. "Maybe we better find his wife first."

"Why's that?" the burly man asked.

"We could use her to control him in case he gets too close. Besides, I understand she pinks like a mink," he added. "Maybe you could look into that and issue a report, eh? Did you find anyone for him?" he asked, turning to the younger man.

"Huh?"

"In Chicago?"

"No, I didn't know no one."

"Well find someone, and give Gus the name. I want you to get close to him so we can pick up any leads. Tell Gus that if he ever needs any help off the job he should give you a call. Tell him you just sit around jackin' off most of the time you're not working, like the Carp, and you wouldn't mind doing something a little more interesting, okay?"

"No problem, boss," the man replied. The idea of infiltrating the enemy struck him as a splendid tactical maneuver.

Spezio relaxed a little, not knowing the extent of Litwak's scheming. He hadn't thought anything of it when Litwak passed him a gun shortly after his wife disappeared, saying, "I just got me a better back-up. What d'you think of this baby?" Spezio had hefted it, sighted along its barrel, and then handed it back, not noticing how Gus carefully took it by the barrel.

A month later Gus dropped three bullets into Spezio's hand in a bar, saying, "Can you tell that these are those cheap Korean imitations? I can't. They look just like the real thing—unless you squint at the tips. But they sure don't pack the same wallop."

Now Gus had the gun with the bullets in it in a plastic bag in a safety deposit box at a branch of the Commonwealth Bank. The only prints remaining on them belonged to Spezio. Of course it was the gun with which Vandelay had been shot.

Gus had been trying to get Spezio to go fishing with him. He had even bought a boat, a 24' Whaler which he kept on a trailer out past Selfridge. Spezio talked about fishing all the time but had resisted going out with Gus, claiming nothing worth reeling in could be found in the toxic wastes of Lake St. Claire.

Gus was preparing to change his tactics. The next time he brought it up he was going to say, "Listen, Richard, I want to talk to you about something, where we won't be interrupted. I, uh, I've been having a little problem with a woman I've been dating. She wants me to try something that I think is kind of sick. But I don't want to seem square, if you know what I mean. You're the most experienced guy I know when it comes to women, so maybe you can give me some advice."

That was something Gus thought Spezio would not be able to resist. When they were sitting out there on Lake St. Claire with their lines disappearing into the mud directly over Vandelay's remains, he planned to hand Spezio a pad of paper and a pencil, and say, "I better adjust the carb on this outboard. Do me a favor while I tune it. Make a map of this fishing spot, would you? Get it as accurate as you can. Use the GPS readings, okay?"

"Why? There aren't any fish here," Gus imagined Spezio replying. Gus had prepared an answer: "That's why. I'm finding the big school by the process of elimination. I'll put your map on my master chart. Initial it, too, so I have a reference. Listen, when I finally track 'em down, you an' me will go out and catch our limit. It'll be like shooting fish in a barrel."

Now, parked down the street from where Spezio was rousting another crack house, sitting in an old car he kept in a garage and never drove to work, he thought over his plan. It made him feel good. It wouldn't be much longer before he'd be ready to spring the trap. The only thing he was waiting for was Sherri; he wanted her to admit what he already knew, just to be doubly sure. Then he would put the gun in Spezio's locker. He had picked up the combination by adroit positioning, one number at a time. And he'd mail the map to the pissheads in Internal Affairs with a note he'd get some clapped-up crack-crazy street-walker to write: 'This where the Speeze say he dumped that fat bigwig's body. He got all the money but he won't give none to me. So this be what he get.'

Seeing the map during the investigation to follow, Spezio would know who had engineered his downfall. That would make it all the better, Gus thought, almost giving in to the urge to grin.

Chapter 7

At work the next day Tony was delighted at how fuddled Bob was. He screwed up the line three times, which earned him a biting reprimand from the supervisor. Ray was in even worse shape. His eyes constantly darted to the main door, as if he were afraid the police might come for him at any moment. Every so often the two of them got together to whisper. One time Tony walked by in an attempt to overhear, but they fell silent until he passed.

The next day both of them were considerably calmer. Tony had mixed feelings. On the one hand he was disappointed their agitation had diminished. He had enjoyed seeing them squirm. On the other hand he thought he might be able to stage the crescendo to his plans after all. Not right away, and only after a controlled encounter with another one of Gina's friends to get Bob to drop his guard again.

After work Tony followed Bob until he saw he was heading to Spuds. He drove around through Toledo's run-down back streets for awhile before coming back and going in. It was the same gang as usual: Bob, Ray, Arnie, and Dave, working on pitcher number two while three women in dungarees took turns stretching to reach the cue ball.

Tony sat down at the bar to bide his time. He tried to catch Arnie's speculation that the rumored TKD buy-out would bring them some decent equipment, but the bald guy next to him kept bugging him to play liar's poker and he lost three dollars before the man would leave him alone. Then Blinky came over, an old drunk who had been born next door to the tavern and still lived there. He fancied himself a comedian and traded jokes for shots. Tony bought him one, even though he couldn't make sense of Blinky's rambling and pointless stories. Who in the hell cared if the mayor's grandfather had put one over on the Toledo and Western railroad?

Finally Arnie and Dave took off; then, Ray, leaving Bob by himself. Tony got two cold Buds and joined Bob at his table. To Tony's surprise Bob treated him as the close friend he had been until that unmerciful ribbing had driven them apart. "You'll never guess what happened," Bob began, spilling out the tale of how a second bound woman had been left at his door.

Tony prodded him for details.

"I decided, hell, the only way Ray's ever gonna believe this is if he has a first-hand experience," Bob said. "So I stopped the tape before I really got into it and ran it back. I put her blindfold on, got her in my car, and drove her to Ray's house. I leaned the poster against her, rang the bell, and hid. Ray took her inside, but before he could get going the cops showed up. I was sitting in the car. Can you believe it?"

"Maybe a neighbor got concerned," Tony offered. "I wondered what you were so worried about yesterday at the shop. You seemed pretty nervous. What'd you tell the cops?"

"I said I was out for a drive, and I started hyperventilating. So I pulled over. They asked me if I needed an ambulance. They were pretty decent about it."

"You're lucky," Tony told him.

"Yeah, don't I know it! Funny thing, some woman called Ray and tipped him off that the cops were on their way. He got so shook up he unstrapped the broad and started apologizing. For a moment he was afraid she was gonna punch him."

"Probably some secretary at the police station who knows Ray. Didn't want him to get into trouble."

"That's what we thought. But last night Ray called a buddy of his on the force to make sure there wasn't any follow-up. We don't want to get our names on some list or anything. This guy, Jake Plummer, said they don't have any lady secretaries on the night shift."

"Maybe one got called in," Tony speculated.

"Jake said not."

"So what d'you think?"

"I don't know. The first woman said her girlfriend had dropped her off, so I thought, maybe she was waitin' for her, and seen me take her in my car and followed me. If she saw me drive her to Ray's, maybe she called him. Just to get her out. They probably studied me and knew I was okay, but they didn't know nothin' about Ray. So this girlfriend could have got worried."

"That must be it."

"But how'd she know Ray's phone number?" Bob asked.

"Maybe she had access to a reverse directory. Like where she works or something," Tony babbled. This was not going as he had anticipated. "They have those, where you can get a name and number for any street address."

"If it was the girlfriend who phoned Ray, how'd she know the cops were on the way?" Bob persisted.

Tony tried to think of an answer, but he couldn't come up with anything that made sense. His heart was pounding loudly in his chest, and his breathing audibly quickened.

"We wondered if maybe she called the police," Bob told him. Tony began to relax, but then Bob withdrew the hope he'd just offered: "But Jake said it was a man who called in the complaint against me. How does that figure?"

Stumped, Tony broke out in a sweat. The song one of the pool players were bopping to came to an end, and an old man with a crutch set his beer down and hobbled over to the juke box.

"I think someone's playing with me," Bob revealed. "And I'm gonna find out who."

"How you gonna do that?"

"Jake is makin' me a copy of the call. They record all of them that come in. Maybe I'll recognize the bastard's voice."

Stunned, Tony's mouth went dry and his heart started to palpitate again. Luckily, Linda and Lois had just come in to celebrate another victorious bowling tournament, and Bob was too distracted by them to notice.

The amazons settled into a booth and began taking inventory. Once their eyes jumped over him without recognition, Bob turned his attention back to Tony, who trotted out one of the comments he had rehearsed: "You should've been satisfied enjoying what you had. You'll be damn lucky if you get a third chance after pulling a stunt like that. Unless maybe she liked it."

He had planned on delivering this in an appropriate context. But the way he threw it in out of desperation made his words sound out of place.

Bob stared at him for ten seconds before replying. "If the doorbell rings again, I sure as hell won't answer it. At least not until I get Jake's tape and get to the bottom of what's going on."

Unnerved, Tony hung around in chagrined silence until it was prudent to leave. Then he raced to Gina's stand in front of the closed-down pharmacy. He was anxious to discuss this turn of events with her; she was far more street-wise. He was hoping she would say the fidelity of the police recording was too poor for identification, or something else to restore his self-confidence.

But she wasn't there. Instead, a pudgy black girl in a bouffant wig and a too-tight red skirt was pacing back and forth like a picket on the line.

Tony slowed to a stop and asked her through the window, "Where's Gina?"

"I'm Gina," the woman replied, bending down to display her cleavage.

"No, the other Gina," he countered. A bubble of anxiety was expanding in his stomach.

"I'm the only Gina here. I'm the only Gina I know. That other bitch was just standin' in for me. I tried to teach her a few things so she wouldn't lose me my customers while I was away, but she only learned a fraction." She held up her stubby hand and measured a quarter inch with her thumb and multi-ringed index finger. "You better have me show you the right way to do whatever she tried. How much she charge you, anyway?"

He drove away, perplexed. He cruised Rose's stand in front of the fur store, but it too was being manned by an unfamiliar face.

The night before, Gina and Rose had been sitting in Wendell's, waiting for Sammi when Midget came in, excited. He'd had three calls in response to the ad he had run.

"You really ran it?" Rose asked.

"You bet! This is just the first day! Wait until the word gets around. We'll be rollin' in dough. I told you girls I could make this work."

Not taking him seriously, they laughed it off. Once Sammi arrived, though, he became more animated and persuasive. Gina noticed how he perked up in her presence, and how she always responded by treating him more demeaningly; she had not lost her sense of what a man required. "I think we should offer fictional heroines, like Scarlet O'Hara, or Marilyn Monroe," he suggested to Sammi. "You can do voices, can't you?"

"Y'all better believe ah cane," Sammi stated in her best Southern drawl.

"I'm thinking of an ending that says, 'I'd really like to do this some more with you, because you're so good. If you want to get together to help me out again, call (800) 555-1234'," he said. "Or whatever. We gotta get a good 800 number."

"I wonder if anyone's taken 800-U-F-U-C-K-M-E yet," Gina queried.

Rose was going to say something, but Midget was on a roll: "Or, 'I'll bet my sister would enjoy this even more than me, and she's got bigger tits too. If you'd like her to pay you a visit, call our 800 number'."

Tink came in and squeezed into the booth.

Even though Midget was persistent, they were used to regarding him as off the wall. But this time Sammi surprised them by arguing his case. The possibility of getting back in the biz without having any of the risks obviously appealed to her, and she came up with a few ideas of her own. "We could have a girl show up with an extra cassette player in her duffel bag and a note saying the guy should put it on for their first session to make sure they're in synch."

"I'll make that tape," Midget volunteered.

"Or Tink," Sammi countered. "He has a deeper voice."

Tink blushed as he stirred his coffee. Midget said he had talked to the three potential customers. He had ruled out the first one as being an obvious nut case. The second was a regular Joe who lived in Vinewood, the same suburb where Gina had been introduced to these dramas on tape. Midget thought this Joe would be more than satisfied with the original scenario.

Rose and Gina protested until Midget explained that Joe had agreed to pay $200. That settled it. Then their only concern was how to split the fee.

They argued back and forth so vociferously that when Alice was pouring them coffee she joked that they should put her in for 10% as long as they were passing out shares. "Then you can forget about payin' for your food," she said. "I'll pick up the check out of my profits."

The mention of a percentage gave Tink an idea. The large man was never given the credit his insights deserved because putting himself forward made him so nervous that people rarely had the patience to hear him out. This time, though, his notion tumbled forth in one clean burst: "We should treat this as a corporation. The five of us are the stockholders, so we get the profit, after expenses. Expenses would be the girl's fee for wearing a tape. She gets $100 every time, okay? Let's make that a rule. Then there's materials. We gotta buy tapes and costumes and who knows what all. Let's say that comes to $20 when we average it out. So if Midget can get $200, we all split what's left. $80, so we each get $16." It was obvious that the platypus was good with numbers.

"That ain't very much," Rose groused. "I'll tell you what, I volunteer to be the first out. I can use the money."

"The third guy's gonna pay $500," Midget announced. "Of course, we gotta make a special tape for him."

"I'll take that one!" Rose announced.

"You already got the other," Gina countered. "This one's mine."

"It don't make any difference," Tink explained. "Whoever goes up to the door gets $100. For this guy, we split up $380."

"Huh?" Gina asked.

"$500, minus the $100, minus $20 for supplies."

"What if supplies are more?" Sammi wondered.

"Then they're more. But if they're not, we each get, uh, $76. Plus the $16 for the other one. So we each net $92."

"If we can run four or five a night...," Rose mused. But the multiplication was beyond her. That was one thing she'd always thought a man was good for.

Midget felt the real key to increasing their earnings would be to get more girls. He almost drooled when the word 'stable' rolled off his tongue. For him, having a stable was the pinnacle of success. He would have rushed out to tell his friends his dream was coming true—if he'd had any.

"And I suppose you wanna be in charge of grooming 'em, eh?" Gina chided. "Rubbing 'em down when they come back from the field? Drying 'em off?"

Rose acted like hiring more girls would be taking money out of her pocket, though, until Tink explained how she'd still get her $100 every time she was left at a doorstep, plus a bigger share of the revenue generated by the larger work force.

"Once we get going, I'll bet women will volunteer to

work for us for free," Midget thought. This was where the action would be.

"Oh sure. I can see some housewife paying us to send her to the husband who's been ignoring her," Sammi kidded. "Expecting his attention to be awakened by the costume and tape."

"Maybe she'll be right," Midget countered.

A spirit of camaraderie settled over them. They finished their coffee, refused Alice's offer of a refill, and got up to go over to Midget's to make the special tape required by their $500 customer. Once they were outside, Sammi had a better idea: "Maybe you two shouldn't come," she told Gina and Rose.

"Why the fuck not?" Gina demanded, thinking I'm not gonna get dumped on again. "We're all supposed to be partners, for Christ's sake!"

"Well, if we get this thing going, then you girls are gonna have to look surprised each time. That's the weak spot in our plan, right there. It's harder to fake surprise than to fake getting off, maybe because when you fake getting off, the guy you're with isn't likely to be critical. Usually his eyes are turning cartwheels, right? So I was thinking, whoever goes to the door shouldn't know exactly what's on the cassette. At least the first time."

"I can come, then, if Gina's going on the call with the new tape," Rose chirped.

"You may get the new tape next time," Sammi

pointed out.

"She's right that we should separate production from operation," Tink put in. "We're production."

"What about Midget? What'll he do? He doesn't have to be there, either, then," Rose complained.

"I need a foil," Sammi told her.

"A what?"

"A dummy to stand there, as if I'm talking to him," Sammi explained.

"That's Midget!" Rose laughed.

"A guy standing there will help make it more real," Sammi qualified herself.

"I don't know," Gina said. "I don't like it. I think we should all be involved in making the tapes. That's the essence of democracy."

"What's the matter, don't you trust me?" Sammi challenged.

"It's not that ....."

"Listen, girlfriend, I'd never send you out with a tape that would get you hurt."

She wasn't sure, but it didn't matter: the issue was decided for them when their ambling down the sidewalk brought them abreast of The Professor, who was sitting in his car with a bag of toys next to him on the seat. His large eyes were both eager and subdued. When Gina saw him, she leaned over to let him talk. "Gina," he moaned. "I'm afraid I've been naughty again."

Rose went back inside to talk to Alice. "Honey, d'you think I could come over to use your sewing machine tomorrow?"

The next night, while Tony was frantically looking for Gina to talk to about the recording the police were going to pass along to Bob, Rose was deposited on a doorstep in Vinewood, bound and gagged. As soon as she disappeared inside, Tink, serving as the designated driver, drove Gina to Provincetown Avenue to deliver her to their more affluent customer.

Midget, sitting in the back and leaning over the front seat, kept chattering away about how rich they were going to be. He'd had three more inquiries but had spent the day looking for a new source for pills and speed and had not had a chance to call anyone back yet. "We need a God-damn car phone," he groused.

"This guy ain't no freak or nothin', is he?" Gina asked.

"He's 60 years old, for Christ's sake!" Midget said.

"That don't mean squat," Gina shot back. "Sometimes they get damn goofy when they get to that age."

"He's a kindly old guy. You're gonna enjoy this, Gina. Trust me."

A shudder ran through her when he said that. She had learned that this was a stock phrase for someone planning a betrayal. Still, she decided to go through with it anyway. It would not hurt to prove her intuition was right one more time.

They parked in front of a locust tree on a broad, crested street in a quiet residential neighborhood near the river, where the driveways of the homes had new cars, RVs, ATVs, and 25' power boats with freshly greased drives and new cabin covers.

Tink was shy about putting the ball in Gina's mouth until she told him it was okay. Midget handed Tink a piece of surgical tape, followed by red lips printed on a different kind of tape. Using a Penthouse as a model, they were as close to the ones Tony had used as Midget's printer friend had been able to come up with on short notice.

Midget passed Tink the placard. Tink helped Gina out of the van, and patiently led her towards a large brick home surrounded by a manicured lawn. Three kinds of daffodils were blooming in a geometric pattern in a bed of black dirt against a house hedged with a rippled plastic fence.

It was just after 10:00 p.m., not quite dark, when Tink positioned her on the stoop. It was protected from the elements by a high-pitched slate roof supported by two stone pillars. She was fastened into a white straight-jacket with her arms secured across her belly by the sleeves bound together in the small of her back. The breast holes were ringed with sequins.

She was wearing a brief pleated skirt, the kind used for cheer-leading or perhaps acrobatics. It barely covered her but was better than nothing. Midget had explained that this would be part of her costume. He had added a designer duffel bag to the repertoire. When she asked him what it was for, in that case, he had answered, "That's where he'll put the money. So whatever you do, don't leave it behind!"

Tink gently fluffed her hair and then applied the blindfold. He asked her one more time if she were okay, prompting a fierce, exasperated nod. Satisfied that everything was as it ought to be, he gave the doorbell three quick rings and then scrambled behind a flowering bush.

A moment later there was some fumbling with the locks, and then the door opened, revealing a tall, thin man of perhaps 70, with tufts of hair above his ears, and translucent blue eyes. He was wearing a grey silk bathrobe over a white dress shirt, and brown Romeo house slippers. He studied his visitor calmly for a moment, and then pompously remarked, "So, you want me to take you back, after all the pain you've caused."

Then his eyes dropped to the placard:

Daddy, I know I let you down. I was a naughty girl. I should have listened to you, and not run away. Please let me come home. I'm willing to pay the price. I promise, I'll never disappoint you again. Just bring me in, remove my blindfold, and push the 'play' button, and I'll tell you what you've been waiting to hear.

His eyes misted over as he read. When he finished, his gaze returned to her face. The muscles in his cheek flexed, as though he had finally bit through something he had been chomping on. "I don't know if I'll ever be able to trust you again," he said. "But I suppose if you've come all the way out here, the least I can do is listen to what you have to say."

He took the placard and duffel inside first, and then came back to guide Gina. Stiffness in his joints impaired his movement. He walked her through the first room and into a second before removing the blindfold.

She looked around. She was in a kind of library with an ornate wooden desk, a fireplace full of carefully arranged artificial birch logs, and expensive furniture: a plush, flower pattern couch, a mahogany coffee table, and two matching leather chairs. There was a small bar to one side on which a half-sipped martini was sitting in a circle of condensation.

"I suppose I should listen to your apology," the man said begrudgingly, pushing the play button and then picking up his drink. "But I'm not going to just forgive and forget, so don't get your hopes up."

A moment later a waif-like version of Sammi's voice issued from Gina's chest: "I'm really, really sorry, Daddy. I should've done what you said."

"It's too late to feel sorry for yourself now," the man replied haughtily.

There was a moment of silence, after which the tape resumed: "Those boys weren't very nice at all, just like you warned me, Daddy."

"You should have listened to me, Sarah."

"I feel really bad, Daddy, because of how they humiliated me," Sammi's voice continued. "They promised to be nice, but once I trusted them they weren't nice at all. The first one took me into his bedroom and pulled his pants down, and made me get down on my knees and do something really dirty. It was terrible, Daddy."

"What did he make you do to him, Sarah?" the old man asked, adjusting himself.

"He wanted me to kiss his penis, Daddy. It wasn't pretty, like yours. I didn't want to do it but he pushed it into my mouth and made me suck on it. He pushed it in and out, and it got bigger and bigger...."

"The brute had no self-control!" the old man exclaimed, speaking over Sammi's voice.

"...and he held my head so tight it hurt. All I could do was try to get it over with as quickly as I could, so I squeezed his balls a little until these bursts just erupted out of him, and then, Daddy, he made me lick up every drop and swallow it. I guess swallowing so much of it made me kind of crazy, because when the next boy came in, I let him put his cock in my mouth too and started gulping on it, even though I knew it was wrong. It was fatter than the first boy's and reminded me of a kind of ugly bulldog or something."

The man set his empty glass in the ring of moisture on the bar and came up to her, putting an arm loosely around her and saying, "There there. Come over here, Sarah. Tell me all about it. Maybe we can figure out an expiation."

He gently pulled her to the couch as the next response started up: "Daddy, it was terrible! I don't know what came over me. The more I swallowed, the more excited I got. I wanted more and more, but they had no idea how to satisfy me, Daddy. They didn't know anything."

"They were just boys, Sarah," the old man cooed, sitting next to her and stroking her hair. "Immature bumpkins. There should be a law prohibiting erections until a man makes a worthwhile contribution to society!"

"No matter what they did, Daddy, no matter where they put their cocks, they kept going off before I was ready. They were pigs. It was just awful."

The old man turned her and pulled her feet over his legs. She squirmed into the position she thought he wanted her.

"I should have listened to you, Daddy. You're the only one who knows how to give a girl pleasure. Going out on my own without you to protect me was a really dumb idea. I hope you'll forgive me and things can be just like they were once again."

"I don't know, Sarah. You really hurt me."

Sammi's voice took a moment to resume; apparently she had anticipated a longer response. "Tell me what I can do to make it up to you, Daddy. I'd give anything if we could do what we used to. I didn't realize how much I would miss it."

"I don't know if I should believe you. I suppose the only way to find out is to give you a little Elmer and see how you react." Gina thought, 'Jesus, not an Elmer'. She would have burst out laughing if she had not been constrained. "If those boys have ruined you, though, I...."

He was interrupted by Sammi: "Please, Daddy, couldn't I have just a little of your good medicine, please?"

"Slide up on my lap, Sarah," the old man said, pulling her over him. He waited until she was sitting on him to reach down and free his penis, as if he didn't want her to see it.

His breathing had grown heavy. He wheezed that she had hurt Elmer's feelings, and would have to be extra nice to make up for that. Sammi kept encouraging him, even after he had found the right place with his nervous, groping hands and guided his rubbery member inside. The way he started to moan gave Gina a frightening thought: 'What the hell would I do if he croaks? Tink and Midget couldn't get in. I'd be stuck here in this pickle until the maid arrives tomorrow morning!'

But the old man didn't die. He pumped gently until he stuttered to a weak conclusion. When he opened his eyes again, Sammi's voice was still encouraging him to hump even harder. He reached over to the player and pushed the off button, and then slid her off his lap.

"That's all we shall need," he said very stiffly, as though he had just concluded a satisfactory but not unduly exciting business transaction.

He reached behind her and unsnapped the Velcro, setting her free. "Thank you very much," he said, not looking at her. "I have something important I must attend to now. I trust you can show yourself out."

When she was back in the van, Tink announced that only 22 minutes had elapsed. "But we got the whole $500!" Midget exclaimed, digging the bills out of the duffel. Then he came up with something else, an ashtray cut from a geode. "What's this?"

"That's my trophy! I needed a little extra for all the humiliation."

Midget and Tink had just returned from picking up Rose, whose session had been routine. "Way to go!" she said, recounting the money. "You've got to tell me all about it!"

"There's not much to tell," she replied. "I feel like I

wasn't really there."

"Honey, I have that same feeling every single time."

Chapter 8

The gang headed back to Midget's apartment in high spirits, where Sammi was to meet them around 1:00 a.m.. Or sooner, if her husband conked out. Rose and Gina took turns telling the two men various details of their experiences.

"I can see why his daughter ran away," Gina exclaimed. "He called his prick Elmer. Like Uncle Elmer. I wonder where that came from? Maybe that was the name of an uncle who took him camping as a kid and taught him how to light a fire by rubbing two sticks together."

"Or Elmer Fudd," Midget laughed. "Always chasing the bunny."

"My guy improvised," Rose said. "He got some baby oil out after he paddled me, and rubbed it into my butt. Round and round, dripping drool on my crack. At one point the tape asked him if he thought it was fair that I was almost naked but he still had his pants on and he screamed, 'Wait a second, I ain't done with this part yet!' He was pissed at the voice interrupting his fun, for Christ's sake!"

"What a dolt!" Midget said. "But, you know what? That's an avenue we should explore— product placement. Now, sir, get a bottle of Johnson's baby oil— it's the only kinds I like."

"At least he was gentle," Tink put in. "I worry about you girls." He glanced fondly at Gina, who was lighting up a cigarette.

"So finally he reached over and pushed the off button, and went and got some talcum powder," Rose continued.

"Please, sir, get some Ponds baby powder," Midget said in a stilted voice.

"Then he got me back on his lap with my butt up, and talked baby talk to me. 'Is my iddle widdle kootchie koo nice and warmie pie?' He began sprinkling and rubbing, sprinkling and rubbing. He got his rocks off just rubbing and sprinkling! He stained his fuckin' pants!"

Tink discreetly adjusted himself, and shot Rose a doe-eyed glance from the driver's seat.

"He never did turn the player back on," Rose said. "After he did his Mount St. Helen imitation he went in the bathroom for ten minutes. I kept thinkin', oh oh, what's this creep gonna do next? But when he finally came out, he half thanked me, half apologized, and set me free."

"I explained to him on the phone that he'd have to set you free at the end of the tape," Midget piped up. "I wanted that clearly understood right from the git-go."

They sat around Midget's drinking beer and talking until Sammi arrived, sporting deep burgundy silk slacks and a matching tie. Then they had to tell their stories all over again. Sammi made Gina go first, keeping the others quiet by motioning with her hand. When Gina finished Sammi made Rose tell her everything she could remember about her experience.

Sammi thought it had gone very well, especially considering the degree of improvising both girls had been forced to do. She counted the money, finding it was all there, and then calculated and passed out everyone's share. As the woman with the most experience, the others accepted her right to take charge—at least for the time being.

"We gotta build on this," Sammi declared.

"Huh?" Midget reacted.

"You were right, Midget. I'll give you that. I think this deal's really got potential, but we gotta take it seriously if we're gonna cash in. We gotta treat it like a business, not just some lark we're on. We can't just fool around."

The others remained silent, waiting for examples.

"We gotta think this through. Gina, what's the future with the old man?"

She didn't grasp the question.

"D'you think we could put him on a regular schedule? $500 for an hour's work would be nice to pick up every week."

"I think we could do it once with Rose. But I don't see him wanting to have me over again. He might have been able to tell what I was thinking."

"We need more girls," Sammi mused. "Maybe if we had three or four, we could cycle 'em back, with different wigs and make-up and stuff."

"You could take a turn," someone suggested.

"Somebody's got to keep their distance," she replied. "If we all become players, we'll start swoopin' in circles. First thing, we'd crash into a wall that nobody was watchin' out for."

"Maybe we could get Alice on occasion. She's barely makin' it on her waitress salary."

"She's the type who's more interested in throwing a birthday party for her puppy," Sammi said. "Plus there's a Jesus fish sticker on her Volkswagen, and I'll bet dollars to donuts there's a Bible verse somewhere that forbids this kind of activity."

"There's a demand for that type too," Midget claimed. "Maybe we could convince her it's a kind of new-age missionary work."

Sammi ignored him, asking Gina if she could think of any ways they could make the tape she had worn better.

Tink remarked that this was like a debriefing. His moment of glory had been as a com-tech in the Gulf War, where he had performed satisfactorily. It hadn't been much, but it had given him the perspective to understand the military approach.

"Not really, it was right on," Gina stated, ignoring Tink.

"You don't know how good that makes me feel," Midget put in. "I mean, I tried hard to capture the dude's fantasy. I think I got a real knack for writing scripts."

Gina gave Midget a disparaging look. "Your voice was pretty darn good, too," she told Sammi. "You had me believin' I was someone else."

"That could be dangerous, girl!" Sammi laughed.

"We should keep records," Tink suggested, still thinking militarily. "Set up a calendar. I've got a lap-top we could use."

"What's that?" Rose asked, envisioning some kind of lap-dancing routine. Gina chuckled, prodded by Rose's tone.

"Good idea. You can be our clerk," Sammi decided.

They fell silent for awhile. Then Sammi asked the group what was next.

"Let's get some coke!" Gina suggested, but Sammi gave her a stern look.

Midget said that tomorrow he would call the three new people who had replied to his ad, and also call the two who Gina and Rose had visited earlier in the evening to see if they wanted to go again. "Maybe I'll offer a 10% discount for repeat business, eh?"

"Ask them to suggest improvements," Sammi directed. "Or, don't ask 'em if they say yes. If it ain't broke, don't fix it."

Tink thought they should put ads in other papers.

"That's a good idea," Sammi praised him, making the big man blush. "Hopefully word of mouth will take over, but until it does we need to up our advertising. That'll be your job, Midget. Director of advertising."

"I thought of it," Tink complained.

"You're gonna have your hands full as our clerk," Sammi soothed him. "But Midget, make sure you tell Tink each time you place an ad. And tell him what it costs. Give him a list of who you call and what kind of guy they turn out to be. He'll need it for his records."

Tink offered to prepare a flow chart showing which ads were the most effective, in regard to both number of calls and profit. He started to explain the capability of his software, but nobody was interested in graphs and pie charts so he let it go.

Seeing his feelings were hurt, Gina broke the promise she had made to herself not to encourage him. Peering into his eyes, she told him earnestly that she thought it was a darn good idea. From that moment on he could not look at her without seeing a goddess. Gina heard a voice in the back of her head say, 'This guy falls in love like someone going over Niagara Falls in a barrel.' She pictured him crammed into a barrel with one little peep hole—in her mind, a good position for men in general.

In the weeks that followed their business grew markedly. They expanded their line of tapes, learned what kinds of ads were the most effective, and developed enough repeat business to have to draft Alice and Poppy, another of the girls from Wendell's, to be able to handle it.

Poppy had a deep, resonant voice, and Sammi began to use her to help make tapes which required a stronger feminine presence. At first it seemed such a role would contradict the very essence of a bound and gagged woman, but they discovered that the opposite was the case. Some men couldn't get enough of being forced to debase themselves by a woman who, strangely, was obviously powerless to enforce her demands. They felt they were tunneling toward the archetype of what modern men had become.

They couldn't quite understand the implications. Sitting around Midget's apartment after a night's work, the five principals frequently speculated about their growing success from different points of view. Sammi was concerned with what impact a particular idiosyncrasy might have on profits. Rose was the one who usually raised philosophical questions, such as whether or not they really wanted to encourage these jerks to do this sort of thing. Gina was more interested in shock value, to add spice to their otherwise repetitive work. If she had a motto to live by it would have to be, If you let life become boring, you're simply a fool.

Tink backed her up. He had become such a kiss-ass that Sammi occasionally rolled her eyes behind his back. Sensing he wasn't being taken seriously this time, Tink insisted that deriving personal satisfaction was as important as making a lot of money, "just like Gina said."

"That's so sweet," Gina responded, leaning forward to kiss his cheek, which required her to support herself by placing a hand on his pulpy thigh. Seeing how she was playing with him, Rose shook her head to indicate she sensed trouble was about to rear its evil, shrunken head.

More and more, Midget said whatever popped into his mind. He might passionately shout something one minute only to contradict himself the next. At times he completely dominated the conversation, but then he turned moody and mute. Rose suspected he was getting into coke, and even thought about asking the girls to stage an intervention.

One night she revealed that her client had complained about how Midget had talked to him on the phone: "'He don't have no respect,' this man said, 'If I was you, little darlin', I'd get me somebody else to answer the calls'."

Sammi, who'd known him the longest, guessed he had gone started using speed. She intended to talk to him about it—if she could just find the time. She was working harder than ever, and doing it on the sly to keep her husband from finding out.

It troubled this successful man that she was spending so much time away from their home. He had awakened in the night twice and not found her there. The first time, he had accepted her excuse of having gone for a walk to cure her insomnia, but the second time he had looked at her suspiciously. "Maybe I'll just break down and get some sleeping pills," she had told him. "At least until I come to terms with whatever old anxiety's tryin' to poke its nose into our new world."

"I'll have my secretary call Dr. Jenkins," he had promised, still wondering. He wished his golfing friend had never said the words that frequently echoed in his mind: 'with a woman that beautiful, you never know what to expect.' He was discovering that his vivid imagination, about which he had always been so proud, could also be a curse.

Yet the sex-and-tape business was growing by leaps and bounds. Word of mouth was finally producing results, and more people than ever were asking for visitations. Midget was so awe-struck by his new self-image as advertising guru that he could not stop drumming up business. They put a plug at the end of each new tape to suggest that if the customer were satisfied he might want to try a celebrity visitation, or a double, or a honeymoon routine. "How about this?" Midget asked. They were sitting around after another successful night. "We can tell our customers they can send one of our girls to a friend? Like, as a birthday present."

"We could print up gift cards," Tink suggested.

"I don't know," Sammi said. "I don't want our girls to go somewhere blind."

"That's always the case anyway. You can never be sure."

"Still, I don't like it."

Just when they were swamped with business, a new possibility occurred which promised to expand it even farther. A satisfied customer who had received Rose at his motel—this was the night when Sammi changed the rules, decreeing that for appointments in public places, or in the daytime, the girls would wear skirts until they were inside—told her, after freeing her hands when he was done, that he was from out of town and couldn't get back very often. If there was any way he could buy a copy of that tape so he could have one of his hometown girlfriends use it, he would be much obliged.

Rose sold it to him on the spot for $100. After all, Tink had made them back-ups, just in case, and in the studio he was assembling with his earnings it was no problem for him to make more copies from the master.

As soon as Tink heard about this he jumped on it: it was a natural! Sammi objected that they could cut their own throat by selling tapes. "Being in the tape-selling business is better than being in direct service," Tink argued, increasingly interested in saving Gina from seamy situations. "We could multiply our market a hundred times. Maybe a thousand! We could tap into areas all over the state—and beyond. Think of the profit!"

"Plus, we don't have to worry about no diseases, selling tapes," Alice put in—their Jesus girl had joined up, but had not made peace with her conscience. Disease was a nagging concern, one of the factors that kept her from deriving as much enjoyment from the calls as the others.

Selling tapes was a beguiling concept. Sammi hated relinquishing control, but she was no fool. She authorized Midget to run a sample ad, just to test the market.

It ran the next day. The response was overwhelming. Apparently word had got around.

Within a week of their first ad to sell tapes, they were moving five or six a day of each of their four basic versions: Please Spank Me, Daddy Dearest, Don't You Dare Not Obey, and I'd Give Anything For More. Tink suggested paying sales tax to protect themselves against federal reprisal. He said he had software that would make it easy. But when he noted the strength of Gina's desire to remain an outlaw, he let it pass.

Purchasers of their tapes sometimes called back with suggestions or special requests. Midget was doing more white powder than ever—whatever it was—but he still could not keep up with the demand for new scripts. Everybody had an angle. Alice saw a TV show about olden times that brought tears to her eyes, and she began bugging Midget to start a historical series. She was dying to go on a call in a lace bodice and mini-hoop-dress. She had always regarded herself as an undiscovered innocent princess.

Sammi came up with the idea of tape sequences: a customer would use one tape on the first night, another on the next, and the last one in the triad on the third. "That way he gets a better experience, because it's cumulative, get it? We can sell three for $199. It would be a good bargain. It'll be like having a guest role in a sitcom."

"If you were using a tape with your girlfriend, and you got bored, it would be easier to get a new tape than a new girlfriend," Midget screeched.

"America's ready for a brand-new addiction," Gina declared.

Rose thought they should offer personalized tapes. Tink said he could get a program that would allow the insertion of a proper name at various points, or even set it up to use a variety of nicknames: Thomas, Tommy, and Tom Tom, for example. Sammi okayed it, telling Midget to offer the personalized versions for $20 more.

When the conversation lagged, Alice told them about a dream she'd had. "I go in, and the guy's wearing one of our straight-jacket costumes and a tape player. He kicks the door shut and pushes my play button with his nose. He's had a visitation before and recorded our tape, and made himself his own tape that answers ours; he's asked for the same one, see. I look around, and everything's hung with tape players. The TV isn't on, but an old show's playing on a tape player. Charlie's Angels, I think it was. There's a tape player on the grandfather clock, ticking away, another on the unplugged coffee maker, gurgling with fresh perk. See, this guy's really into it; his whole world's on tape."

"Could happen," Rose confidently declared.

"Already has—in California," Gina joked.

On his own Midget placed ads for tapes in papers in other nearby cities. He did not want to say anything until he saw how it went. Even though his mind was going a mile a minute he had no idea what to expect. On the one hand, their offering was a novel idea, and novelties usually did well, at least for a while. But on the other, without the advantage of first familiarizing the clientele through personal visitations, he did not know if it would have any appeal. He half-expected every possible outcome to occur simultaneously; he had quantum theory on his brain

He need not have worried. Phone calls and face to face conversations had created enough awareness in Cleveland, Akron, and Cincinnati that inhabitants of those towns jumped at the tapes, perhaps to make up for the lack of a local visitation service. Soon the tape sales part of their business was booming to such an extent that

Sammi instructed Midget not to make appointments for Tuesdays and Thursdays; she needed the entire crew to help make the many suggested new tapes.

Rose and Poppy were neutral, but Alice was overjoyed. She had gotten involved only to help her friends and had never been comfortable with the idea of being bound and gagged and deposited on a stranger's doorstep. She was terribly afraid that the customer would turn out to be someone she knew—like her minister. Plus, a lot of the men she had been sent to were types she did not at all like.

But Gina was pissed. She had always railed against the impersonality of big business and much preferred the one-on-one interaction of the visitation. Living by her wits in situations fraught with danger gave her an addictive stimulation; it's what she did, what she took pride in. "Jesus Christ, next we'll be punching a fuckin' time clock," she groused to Tink when he drove her home.

He did not say anything, because the thought that came to him was too exciting for him to be able to control his speech: maybe the two of them should branch out and start their own business. He could handle the ads, the phone calls, and the bookings. Gina could make the tapes. Together they could put together a stable of women to make house calls. Once they had all returned, he and Gina could call it a night, go to bed, and sleep in the next day, only getting up in time to catch the bank before it closed.

Chapter 9

The local cops began to worry. They'd heard that a new service was moving in, although its customers were unusually secretive about the details. The cops had nothing against new business, but so far nobody had approached them to discuss how they would get their share. That was downright disrespectful.

The captain sent a memo to the vice squad, asking them, in the appropriate jargon, to put more pressure on this operation whenever they had the chance. 'I shouldn't take it personally,' he told himself. 'They probably just don't know. A few nights in jail oughta get their attention.'

"They're soliciting business with ads in the paper," one of the vice cops told the captain, catching him in the hall. "You want us to set up a sting?"

"Not yet. The boss is scared shitless when it comes to violating the fuckin' First Amendment. Look what the Garafolos did to those narcs; they're out walkin' a fuckin' beat! Besides, when you do a thing like that, everybody finds out. It could do more harm than good. Remember the time the State Police got in the middle of that cock-fighting ring we were working? It didn't seem like much money, did it, until we stopped getting it. Anyway, just keep your eyes open for the time being."

Jake Plummer, Ray's friend on the force, had asked

his sergeant about making a copy of the phone call that had resulted in a car being dispatched to Ray's house the previous month, but the sergeant vetoed it. Ray had hinted to Jake about having received a woman under unusual circumstances. "Those boys are just playin' practical jokes," the sergeant had said when Jake passed on the news. "Giving them a copy of our recording would only lead to trouble. We don't want this thing to accelerate."

One night at softball practice, Pete Garitty, an older cop confined to first base by his limited range, was talking to Jake about the captain's memo while they waited to bat. "They're acting with impunity," he said. "That's a fuckin' insult. We're gonna squeeze 'em a little, see if we can get 'em to toe the line."

Jake wondered if these might be the same people who his friend Ray had encountered six weeks earlier. Pete asked about the details, but Jake couldn't remember much.

"Maybe I better go see this guy," Pete thought.

"Let me have him call you," Jake urged. "He told me some things in confidence, and I don't want to turn around and sic the dogs on him."

"Bark bark bark."

Jake called Ray and asked him to phone Pete. Ray drank a six-pack, worrying through his options. When he finally decided to make the call, Pete asked him to meet him at Malloy's for a beer. "On me."

Malloy's had come full circle. It had been built as a tavern at the end of the nineteenth century, and had operated as such until Big Mike Malloy was hit by a filament of lightning. He survived, but his hair turned white and he found God in the sparks. Soon the tavern was converted into a Malloy's grocery store, but the human light bulb devoted his energy to the revival circuit with a predictable result: his business went under.

Next it was taken over by a family of Polish immigrants. They baked their own bread and canned their own jams. The enterprise flourished until Europe divided in 1914. They announced it would be better to die like lemmings for the homeland than to cower in safety in America. Those who disagreed with their choice of sides, or were angry over the demands to pay off their account that arrived from overseas, expressed their wrath against the empty building with hammers, pikes, and axes.

After it was rebuilt it became a branch of the Post Office. For awhile it did a banner business in three-penny blues. It closed during the Depression—people didn't send as many letters then because nobody liked to get bad news. A man with a flare for gabardine but no business sense reopened it as a custom haberdashery, and quickly became Toledo's best-dressed failure. Then it did duty as a camera shop, a hardware store, and a hair salon. Each of its new owners were full of enthusiasm, which inevitably gave way to the bleak economic reality of the times. Toledo always missed out when a Renaissance swept through the rest of Ohio.

Now it had come full circle and was a bar again, operated by a man with a good enough pension to not have to worry about making a profit. Plus, he was wise enough to just pay the various fees requested of him and shrug it off. He wasn't looking for a fight.

Ray had never been there but knew where it was. Garitty was waiting when he arrived. The two men took a table, with the cop sitting so he could watch the door. "This is off the record, right?" Ray asked.

"We just want to figure out what's goin' on," Pete assured him, calling for a pitcher.

Sweating and squirming, Ray related the whole story of how Bob's doorbell had been rung and Bob had found a woman on his stoop, trussed and gagged and with a cassette player around her neck. How Bob had told him about it later that night. How, when it happened again with a different woman Bob had brought her to his house to prove his story.

"What'd she charge?" Pete wondered.

"Nothing! She just liked the kinky stuff."

"Come on, you can tell me," Pete wheedled.

"No shit, Pete! She was free!"

Pete told him that maybe she hadn't charged him, but

the group that had sprung up was charging everyone else. "You were probably just a test run," he concluded.

Pete asked Ray to call Bob and get him to come down to Malloy's to talk to him. "I'd rather you call than me," Pete said. "I don't want him to feel anxious. We're only gathering information. This'll be a big help to us."

Bob joined them a half hour later, nervous as a thief. Pete Garitty ordered a second pitcher of beer and got him to relax by telling him about a woman who nipped off a little skin when she gave guys a blow job, blaming her braces if the guy complained. "When we finally busted her we discovered she was assembling a trophy penis in her apartment, bit by bit," Pete fibbed. "She saved each piece and added it to her collage the next day. Molded it on a big black dildo she'd ordered from Africa. She had the trophy mounted above a bronze plaque containing a list of all the guys' names."

At first Bob was reluctant to say much, but when he realized Pete just wanted to hear his story he began to loosen up. He told him about his experience in detail, becoming somewhat boastful in answering Pete's questions.

"She didn't ask you for money?" Pete queried.

"No! The subject never came up. Of course she had her mouth taped shut, and the only words were the ones on the tape."

"Still, they could've asked for money on the tape,"

Ray loyally pointed out.

"You never saw either of these girls before, or since?" Pete wanted to know.

He looked at each man in turn; both said no, with Ray emphasizing that he had never seen the first. Pete asked if they might be able to identify the women from mug shots. They didn't know. They'd been in costume, Bob said, and in any event he hadn't really studied their faces.

"Well, I guess that's it," Pete said, pushing his chair back. "Call me if you think of anything else, or if it happens again."

"Here's something that may help," Bob told him. "One of the guys at work told me it happened to him too."

"You never mentioned that," Ray said. "Who was it?"

"Tony Brancusi."

"He's a real dong," Ray volunteered. "A real creep. He acts like he's better than us."

Pete's interest was reawakened. He asked Ray if he'd call Tony and ask him to come down to Malloy's, but Ray begged off—"I'm not buddies with him."

Pete looked at Bob, who leaned back and raised his hands to chest height, with his palms out—the universal symbol of not wanting to have anything to do with something. So Pete went to the pay phone in the hallway leading to the bathroom, got Tony's number from the operator, and made the call himself.

Tony became jumpy as soon as Pete Garitty identified himself. Pete told him he was just getting information about a new ring of hookers who used bondage and taped messages, and waited for Tony to volunteer what he knew. Instead, the receiver emitted only the sound of Tony's raspy breath. "I understand you had an experience with one of these girls," Pete prodded.

"No, I didn't," Tony told him.

"You told Bob Arkin you did," Pete confronted him.

"I, uh, I just said that, uh, so he'd tell me what happened to him," Tony replied, anxious to conclude the conversation. "He had an encounter. Actually, two. He's the one you should ask."

"What'd he say?" Bob asked when Pete sat back down. "Was it the same girl?"

Pete told them that Tony had claimed he had only said it had happened to him to get Bob to tell him about his experience.

Ray rolled his eyes. "Fuckin' weenie," Bob remarked.

Pete ordered a new pitcher for Ray and Bob but left before it arrived. Driving home, he thought over what he had been told. It didn't amount to much—just another kinky angle on the world's oldest scam. He was never surprised at how weird things had become in the modern world. As a novelty it might run a while longer, he thought. But novelties did not have a good track record. Chances were, if they left it alone it would go belly up soon enough. And if it did not, they would start taking their share.

Turning onto Division Street, he heard a replay of Tony's voice and suddenly realized it was very close to the voice they'd recorded when the call came in that resulted in an officer being dispatched to Ray's house. A surge of excitement swept through him and he said to himself, 'I love it when a plan comes together.'

He changed direction and drove to the station. After all, nobody was waiting for him at home; he had the typical cop's reaction to marriage: been there, done that. Playing the recording again confirmed his suspicion: this screwball was the one who had made that call! Pete punched his name into the department's computer, hoping for a rap sheet, but Tony was clean. 'A solid citizen,' Pete mused. 'They're the most fun to squeeze.'

Pete got back in his car and headed for Tony's apartment on Grant Street. Tony started quaking in his boots when Pete Garitty showed him his badge and asked to come in.

"I talked with you on the phone awhile ago," Pete said. "But you weren't honest with me. So I decided to come over so we could straighten this out face to face. I want to tell you that no crime has been committed. We're only investigating this new ring to get a handle on it on before it gets out of hand. But I need you to tell me the truth."

"What d'you mean, I wasn't honest?" Tony asked, hating Bob more than ever for siccing this policeman on him. This wasn't going his way.

"We know you phoned the police about a man sitting outside of Raymond Cronin's home. That man turned out to be Robert Arkin, another one of your friends from work."

Several possibilities raced through Tony's mind but each one fragmented before he could launch it as a reply. His nerves tingled, and he experienced a sudden loss of mass. Feeling the heat of the policeman's gaze, he asked, "Do they know it was me?"

"There's no reason they have to," Pete assured him. "As long as you cooperate. We aren't trying to create a feud or anything. I could care less what kind of joke you were playing on your friend. Sending him a hooker's just one step up from ordering him a half dozen pizzas. That's what this is when you strip away the fancy props: just a flock of hookers with a different angle. Near as I can tell, when Bob took the second girl over to Ray's house, you called the police to break it up. No big deal. You probably thought you were saving her from something she hadn't bargained for, right? Maybe you thought you'd have to pay extra. Is that it?"

Tony's eyes jumped over the moon.

Pete adopted a soothing tone. "I just want you to tell me anything you can about their operation. Off the record."

Tony felt a surge of gratitude over the camaraderie conveyed by the policeman's voice. But the idea that Gina and Rose were being regarded as a ring of hookers made him apprehensive. He didn't want to implicate himself as their founder. So in the story he told, he said he had stopped down by the old train station to find a hooker he could hire to pay a call on Bob out of the blue, and the one he had chosen suggested the bondage and taped message.

"How did you make the tape?" the policeman asked.

"She made it," Tony lied. "She already had it when I picked her up."

"And the second girl?"

"That was Rose. She was Gina's friend. Of course, that's probably not their names. Bob bragged so much about how he'd enjoyed the first woman that I decided to do it again."

"What'd she charge? That must've been a pretty expensive practical joke."

"Uh, a hundred bucks."

"You're lucky. You got off cheap. Depending on what you want you can easily spend a lot more. You didn't happen to hear anything else, did you?"

"Like what?"

"Like who's behind this, or how many girls they have in their corral? They're into drugs, I suppose. And they aren't paying their taxes, as far as we can tell."

Tony said he had told him all he knew. Pete seemed satisfied. He gave him his card and asked him to call if he thought of anything more. In response to Tony's question Pete reassured him he would not betray his identity. "We always protect our sources," Pete said. "You'd be surprised how many people call us when they hear something. It may only be once or twice a year, but that's enough for us to know we owe them. So we have to make sure nothing ever leaks out. You understand what I'm saying?"

Tony nodded, unable to speak because of the anxiety that came from realizing he was now on the hook, and this cop would do everything he could to keep him there as long as he could. 'Shit, shit, shit,' he silently swore.

"Maybe tomorrow, stop down to the station, would you? We'd like you to look at some pictures, see if we can put names on these butts."

In his mind Tony swore a blue streak as he felt himself slide down the slippery slope.

Chapter 10

The way Tink mooned over her was making Gina nervous. He was definitely crimping her style. Sitting in Midget's dingy apartment during yet another brainstorming session, she looked over at the big galoot. An idea flitted across her mind: maybe I should do the fucker just to get him off my back.

Actually, the whole situation was becoming much too controlled to suit her. 'I might as well get a 9 to 5,' she found herself thinking. 'And who the fuck made Sammi the boss?'

Midget was telling a story that Poppy had supposedly told him—although they all were aware of his predilection to turn a casual comment into a full-blown drama. According to Midget, he'd had a late call for a visitation from a guy out in Sixpence, a newer neighborhood on the south side of town marked by half-round second-tier windows, wave after wave of undulating vinyl siding, and curved, ambling cul-de-sacs planted with tall aspen and spruce. The guy wasn't particular about what tape the girl wore. He said he'd heard about their service and wanted to check it out. When Midget told him no one was available he offered to double their fee.

So Midget called Poppy, who wasn't supposed to work that night. She had just been sitting around watching the HBO movie, though, so she agreed to let him pick her up. She suited up on the way to Sixpence, and he had her in position on the designer stoop by 10:45.

The man opened the door and helped Poppy inside. When he removed her blindfold she saw something that stopped her in her tracks: another bound woman, staring helplessly as the tape in the player tied around her waist droned away in a teasing voice, "Oh, darling, you really know what I need. You know how much I want to watch you screw another woman, and have another woman watch you screw me."

Without batting an eye the man replaced Poppy's tape with one from his personal collection. Then he serviced whoever's tape begged for attention the most fervently.

"Jesus Christ!" Sammi exclaimed. "We can't allow that!"

"Relax," Midget cautioned. "It wasn't no competitor's tape or nothing. After the guy set Poppy free she found out the other woman was his wife. He'd made both tapes just for his own private use. Got his secretary at work to do the voices."

"Still ...," Sammi mused.

"I almost went back in to offer him a job working for us," Midget concluded. "Poppy said the tapes were really good. Oh, I talked to Sophie about comin' to work for us."

"Sophie?"

"You know, the Spanish girl that just got out of rehab."

"I didn't give you permission to do that."

"Lighten up! She turned me down. Said it sounded unnatural. She told me I would go to hell for such perversion. I guess she had a religious experience in the joint."

There's gonna be trouble, Gina thought. The idea excited her, although it was the epitome of a useless intuition: it gave her no clue about which direction to watch for this vector of impending disruption. Halfway to brilliant, the story of her life.

All day long Tony was nervous about going down to the station. He was worried that he would be recognized and people would wonder what he was doing there. He didn't want to do it but he didn't want Pete to come to his apartment again either.

Finally he decided to just get it over with. 'If anybody asks, I'll say I witnessed a hit and run,' he told himself.

He got there at 4:30 and sat out in front for ten minutes to get control of his breathing. Whatever pictures Pete showed him, he resolved not to identify Gina or Rose. Particularly Gina. He had found himself thinking about her more and more. He had begun to believe she must have developed a respect for his intellect because he had surprised her with his request. He was hoping fate would allow him to pursue this relationship.

Inside the police station, Pete shook his hand warmly and thanked him for coming. He complained about the weather as he led Tony to a small office, where he motioned for him to sit down at a desk littered with forms and faxes and then placed an album of mug shots in front of him. Pete lit a cigarette and sat off to the side with the sports page from the newspaper while Tony leafed through the pictures.

After awhile Pete noticed Tony was staring at one of the faces. "Find her?" he asked, rising and coming over.

"No, but here's a girl I used to date, four or five years ago. Maria Jimenez. What'd she do? She doesn't look so good. She used to be quite pretty."

"Her? Same old, same old. I should take that picture out. She's been dead for two years. Bad way to go. First they cut off her titties. Then they made her eat 'em. Finally they cut her throat. She bled out in the gutter."

Tony quickly flipped the page.

Chuckling silently at the gullible sap, Pete went back to the paper. He had already read it at lunch. But he had learned that people gave more information if they relaxed and felt safe, so he tried to make his presence as unobtrusive as possible.

When Tony finished the book Pete brought him another, and then a third. But he did not pick out any of the faces. "She's probably new in town," Pete remarked. "She just ain't been busted yet."

Tony closed the last book. There was a knock at the door, followed by a manila envelope being passed in by a disconnected hand. Pete took it and tore it open, finding a mimeographed letter and two glossy 5 x 7 photos of an attractive woman. He threw one on the desk, saying, "It ain't her, by any chance?"

Pete had not looked at Tony, but something about the man's sudden absolute silence drew his inner eye.

"N...no, n...not her," Tony said.

'Well I'll be damned,' Pete said to himself. 'Sometimes you just get lucky.' To Tony he simply apologized for having wasted his time and thanked him for coming in.

Tony rose, shook hands more energetically than the situation called for, and left, buoyed by the illusion that he had fooled the police and was home free.

At the end of June something happened that made Alice quit. She had been on a two-nights-a-week, two-sessions-a-night shift, and was gradually overcoming her reluctance—thanks in part to the $2300 she had put in the bank from her work.

Midget got a call in the afternoon from Kent Village, an affluent area on the east bank of the Maumee. The person asked for a visitor with the I'd Give Anything For More tape, which was one of their most popular numbers. It was one of Alice's nights to work at Wendell's, but everyone else was booked so he penciled her in and then went to her tiny apartment to talk her into it. "It'll only take an hour," Midget coddled.

"I hate myself for being so easy," she scowled, agreeing.

"All you need to do is get someone to cover for you from 10:00 until 11:00," he said. "We'll pay them—it won't come out of your pocket. Pomi will drop you off and pick you up," he added, referring to their new employee, Pomi Punchali, a college student with a station wagon whom Tink had met at Radio Shack. He was either Indian or Pakistani, short, and hard to understand, but well-intentioned and honest to a fault. The girls accepted him because he worked hard and laughed uproariously at their jokes, no matter how feeble they were. Rose liked to tease him about taking his pay in trade.

"Pomi?" Alice said, disparagingly.

"Pomi's okay," Midget assured her. But her expression made him wonder. "Isn't he?"

"I suppose. It's just that he always wants me to tell him all the details of what happened, and I'm doin' my best to forget it. I think he's writing a book."

"I'll talk to him, okay? He'll pick you up at ten."

The house in Kent Village was spectacular. It had a picket fence, a flagstone facade, and the kind of multiple roof that was composed of a sequence of gables sitting on top of each other like a pagoda village. There was an attached three-stall garage with a basketball hoop, and four or five pine trees in the front yard. Impressed, Alice asked Pomi what he thought it had cost.

"At least in the approximation of $285,550," he told her in his dancing English.

Then it was time for her gag. He patted it down, picked up the placard and duffel bag, and walked her up to the ornate entry door with its amber oval window. Once she was there, he put on her blindfold.

Back in his station wagon, he called the house from his cell phone. This was a change in procedure he had suggested, which Sammi had approved; the placards were just too cumbersome. When his call was answered he clicked a button, and a pre-recorded message in Sammi's pleading voice came on: "Would you please come to the door, and let me in? I can't wait to get underway. Once I'm inside, remove my blindfold and press my play button."

A moment later the door opened, and Alice disappeared inside. Pomi sat there scrunched forward to read one of his engineering textbooks by the dash light and compulsively poke at his tea-stained teeth. Other students in his class found the information on deflections in a steel beam interesting, but he hated having to memorize these things. The more he read, the more he found himself dreaming of ways in which he might change his life and inject it with a little joy. As it was, his future offered only boredom and drudgery.

He was lost in one of his recurring daydreams of a better life and didn't notice the front door open 45 minutes later, or Alice run out in tears. She ripped off her lips and threw them on the lawn as she sprinted towards the car. And although she had grabbed the duffel—Sammi had drilled it into her head that that's where the money would be, and any girl who failed to bring it back would be punished—she had not taken the time to slip into her skirt.

"Get going!" she demanded, jumping in. "Get me out of here!"

Pomi fumbled with the key, asking, "What has happened? Are you being all right?"

"It was a woman!" she screamed.

Pomi managed to get the engine started. "What do you mean by saying that?" he asked, driving away. "How could it be a woman? Surely that is not possible."

"It was a woman!" she screamed again, dissolving in tears. "Take me home!"

"I am instructed to drive you to Midget's apartment now," he protested.

"Take me home or I'll get out of the car right here and walk," she demanded.

He tried to get her to talk but she would not respond.

She sobbed silently and cradled herself in her arms. Despite her order he drove to Midget's and stopped. "We should really go inside to tell Midget what has happened," he said.

"No! I told you to take me home!"

"I do not know where it is that you are living," he explained.

She directed him. It was only a few blocks away. Solicitous, he kept apologizing to her.

"Right there," she said, pointing at a dumpy bungalow next to a laundromat.

She started to get out, and only then realized she had not put her skirt on. She closed the door and slipped it on and then, glancing at Pomi's glasses and pock-marked face, asked him to come in for fifteen minutes. "I've got to take a shower and wash all that filth off me," she stated. "I don't want to be alone. I might freak out. Then you can take me to Wendell's, okay?"

Pomi grabbed his book. When she went into the bathroom and locked the door with an audible click he phoned Midget to explain what had happened.

"Are you sure it was a woman?" Midget asked him, trying to recall the voice that had placed the order.

"I did not see her but that is what she has repeatedly maintained!"

"Okay, okay."

"What would you wish for me to do?"

"Just do what she says. Call me once she gets to Wendell's. I'll have Sammi come down and talk to her."

"I should receive much extra remuneration if you wish for me to stay there until then. Is that not right?"

"Do whatever she asks. Don't worry about your extra. You're a good man, Pomi, and we wanna do right by you," he said. But he did not like being pushed by the finicky little Hindu, and resolved to replace him as soon as he could.

Sammi got to Wendell's at 1:45. Behind the counter, Alice was back at work. After saying hello to her friends Sammi took the back booth, and asked Alice to join her for a cup of coffee when she had a chance.

When Alice sat down Sammi began earnestly apologizing. "I'm truly, truly sorry," she said. "That God-damned Midget ought to be able to tell a man from a woman."

"That's okay," Alice replied. "I was real shook up about it at the time. It felt like being raped, but I've put it behind me now."

"I'm really sorry," Sammi said. "Here, here's a bonus for having gone through what you did." She pushed an envelope containing $200 across the table—her $100 fee, plus the balance of what they'd collected at Kent

Village. Alice tried to refuse it but Sammi insisted, saying they didn't deserve a penny because they had not done their job right.

Alice finally took it, and thanked her. She interrupted Sammi's continuing expression of sympathy by announcing that she did not want to do this any more.

"I understand," Sammi said. "But don't decide right now. Take a few days to think it over. We'll cover everything until the weekend. Then we'll sit down together and talk this over."

"Okay," Alice agreed. "But I've made up my mind and I won't change it. I just couldn't go back. I'd always be worried that this could happen again."

"I'm really proud of how you handled this," Sammi told her. "If it had been me I might have gone ballistic! Once the client set me free I would have scratched her eyes out."

"I wanted to," Alice admitted, glad for the support.

"It seemed like such a nice neighborhood, too. I drove by before I came here to see for myself. You just can't tell anymore."

"I guess there's perverts everywhere," Alice said.

"I guess so. What'd she do, anyway?"

"I'd rather not talk about it," Alice pouted.

"I understand. But what did she look like? I mean,

was she dressed like a man, or anything?"

"Not really. Well, kind of. She was wearing like a smoking jacket or something. But I knew it was a woman as soon as she took the blindfold off. I thought to myself, Jesus, this guy's got his wife to help him get me ready. I was such a fool!"

"No you weren't, Alice. Who could have known?"

"She took me into some room where the lights were real low and music was playing. Karen Carpenter, I think. She had some white stuff that she rubbed on me. In certain places. She said it would help me relax, but it had the opposite effect."

"Some kind of coke?"

"I never saw coke like that before."

"Then what did she do?"

"Well, she started talkin' about how greedy men were. About how they didn't care if a woman enjoyed herself or not. She had that right, anyway. She turned on a video with two women makin' out. She said it was just to show me how good one woman could make another feel. I was real nervous. I thought I was gonna throw up."

"What'd she do next?"

"She pushed the play button, and then your voice started telling her that I needed to be taught how to behave and all, you know. She sat there on her couch watching me for maybe ten minutes. She told me to do a little shimmy. Like I was trying to get my boyfriend hot. She had a riding crop or something in her hand. She started nudging me with it, and I thought she'd beat me if I didn't do what she said. I kept counting down the minutes in my head."

"Then what?" Sammi asked.

"Well, she said, 'You're givin' me a real boner, honey.' I thought she was crazy. But she pulled aside her jacket, or bathrobe, whatever it was. Just for a second. She really did have a boner! It was surreal!"

"She had a penis?"

"Well, it turned out it was just rubber. Or something. But the first look of it sure seemed real. She flashed it a few times while she talked back to the tape. She was gettin' herself worked up. Hypnotized. Then she took off her robe and greased herself up, and got me onto the couch ...." Tears formed in her eyes, which she was having difficulty holding back.

"There, there," Sammi soothed her. "Let's not talk about it any more. I'm really sorry about this. If I could think of some way to make her pay, but, well, you know how hard it is to get back at rich people, right? You did a very good job, though, especially under such unexpected circumstances. Listen, you need anything? Rose said she'd stay with you for a couple of days if you'd like."

"No, I'm gonna be okay. I guess I didn't get no broken bones or nothin'. I'll get over it."

"I'm so proud of you, Alice," Sammi cooed, rising. "You're a real trouper."

"You know what the worst part is?"

Sammi shook her head.

"Whenever I close my eyes, I see her pull her robe back to show me that thing. The way she smiles, she thinks she has complete power over me. She rode me for what seemed like an hour, and all the time she kept sweet-talking with her lips on my ear. Then when I started to come she pulled out and said I wouldn't get any more until I asked for it. So I did, but all she did was tickle me a little with it and said she couldn't hear me, so I asked again. Finally she put it in and finished me off. Afterwards she got this sneer and told me when I came back I'd have to pay her. That was the worst part."

Walking outside, Sammi said to herself, 'well, well; I think we've stumbled on a whole new market. This could be a veritable gold mine.'

Alice had followed her through the door. "I mean, for me to pay her, I'd have to take money out of my mail-order seminary fund," she said. "That's nothing I'd ever do. It's certainly not what Jesus would have done."

Chapter 11

Back in Detroit, Gus Litwak got Pete's phone call just after he had climbed into bed in his dreary apartment on DeQuindre. He had been listening to Margaret Stormhauser extol the virtues of Riverdance, which she wanted him to take her to the following weekend, and he assumed she was calling back with yet another reason why he should.

It was a man, though. He didn't give his name, or say where he was from—Gus's caller ID gave him the number, which he was able to identify as a phone booth at a service station in Toledo once Pete hung up.

"You're lookin' for a certain woman?" Pete asked, holding a paper towel from the gas station's bathroom over the acrylic mouthpiece.

"You found her?"

"Not sure. What's she done?"

"She cleaned out my bank account when she took off on me," Gus shouted.

"Did you press charges? Is she wanted?"

"She's my wife, God damn it!"

"Just askin', buddy. Is there a reward?"

"She wiped me out, man. All I've been able to put

173

aside is $1200, but you're welcome to it if you can tell me where she is."

"What d'you wanna do to her?" Pete asked. "I don't wanna be involved if you're out for revenge."

"Just talk to her," Gus said. "I know this is crazy, but I still love her. I'm hoping we can work it out. I'm willing to forgive her if she'll just come home."

"I'll get back to you."

"Wait!" Gus yelled—but the line had already gone dead.

Gus got out of bed and poured himself a drink. 'So she's in Toledo,' he said to himself. Then he pushed some buttons on the device that recorded all his incoming calls, and sat on the edge of the bed to listen to a replay.

The casual-seeming tone and controlled enunciation struck a familiar chord. 'The guy's a fuckin' cop!' Gus thought after hearing the call twice again.

Gus was part of a stake-out the next day so he could not take sick leave and drive to Toledo until the day after. He packed his suitcase to get ready, and included a copy of the call he had received. If nothing else developed, he planned to go to the vice cop he had mailed Sherri's picture to and play it for him. It did not seem right to be shaken down by a brother officer.

Lieutenant Spezio was unsure what to do. Ever since

he had learned Gus was hunting for his wife he'd had a tap on his phone, using the police facilities. He too knew the call had come from Toledo. But he could not go running off on a wild goose chase every time a tip came in. The young militia-type who had gotten close to Litwak at Spezio's command had not reported anything being up. Most likely this caller was just some scammer who had seen Sherri's picture and figured with a woman like her, there would have to be a healthy reward.

Yet the voice sounded more solid than that. After ten minutes of pondering, Spezio decided to call the number back. It rang and rang. Finally, after 42 rings, an attendant went over and picked it up: "Yeah? What the fuck d'you want?"

Spezio was aware this was a different voice. "There's some money in it for you if you can tell me who made the previous call," he said.

"How much?"

"A hundred bucks."

"I don't know his name. He's a cop, and he drives a jazzed-up gold Blazer. The big model. Now how do I get my money? Hello? Hello?"

Spezio drove over to Carpenter's apartment in Royal Oak, a working-class suburb on Detroit's north side. He wanted to tell his henchman what he had learned. As he expected, Carpenter had fallen asleep in his Barca-lounger watching one of the XXX tapes from his large personal collection.

"What's up, boss?" Carpenter asked, rubbing his eyes and hitting the 'off' on his remote. He was a large man, gone to paunch. He walked with a limp, and had several other wounds and injuries from the abuse he had taken for the department over the years. He did not expect them to make this right on their own. But Spezio understood and was helping, which was why Carpenter felt such a strong bond of loyalty.

"Pack your bags, Carp," Spezio told him. "We're going to Toledo."

"What the fuck's in Toledo?"

"Just a loose end. We gotta take care of it, or we might not get to enjoy the fruits of all our labor." Carp smiled; this sounded like something he would like.

Tink was waiting for Gina outside a modest bungalow on Toledo's northwest side, a large cottage with leaded windows and a steep roof. She was trying a new routine that she and Poppy had worked up, which required two tape players and a mannequin. The whole idea seemed foolish to Tink, but he had been outvoted. He did not like it, and worried that something might go wrong. He was trying to think of the best way to tell Gina about his plan.

He'd had to carry over the cumbersome mannequin. It had the same gaudy lips, its wig was glued on, and it was dressed in shiny black leather. Then he came back to help Gina to her usual position. He dialed the customer on his cell phone from his van, and played a pre-recorded message: "Hi. We're here. Open your door, and bring me in first. I'm the one wearing leather. I'm in complete charge, right? As soon as I'm set up, push my play button. Now do as you're told, dummy, and make it snappy."

Poppy had supplied the mannequin's voice, and Sammi Gina's. When the man brought the mannequin in and pushed its 'play', Poppy's voice demanded that he agree to do exactly what she said. Once he had, she told him, "bring the fleshy slut in. She's been very bad, and you're going to have to teach her a lesson."

The man opened his door and carefully helped the blindfolded Gina inside. He seemed in his mid-40s, and had good posture and translucent blue eyes. He reminded her of that Norwegian tennis star she'd seen on the Late Show.

"Remove her blindfold," the mannequin ordered. "And push her 'play' button ... now!"

A few minutes of synchronized repartee followed, between Miss Toughclit—the leather-clad mannequin—and Little Dripcunt—Gina. The man was left out. Then Miss Toughclit explained the situation to the customer: "Little Dripcunt here has become quite a tease. She thinks she can wiggle her butt in front of one guy after another without having to face the consequences. That doesn't seem right to me. Does it to you?"

"No, it doesn't," the man whined, adjusting himself.

"How would she like it if a guy just teased her, without letting her get off?"

"She wouldn't like that at all," the man said.

"I think it would serve her right, though, don't you? Oh, and always address me as Miss Toughclit. You got that?"

"Yes, Miss Toughclit. And I do think it would serve her right, like you said. Miss Toughclit."

"Take your pants off, so Little Dripcunt can see what she's missing," the mannequin ordered.

The man complied, folding them neatly over a chair. "My underwear too?" he asked. The question was ignored but he took his kangaroo-pattern boxer shorts off anyway and carefully placed them on top of his slacks.

"I happen to know that what Little Dripcunt really likes is to get poked from behind," the mannequin confided. "Now ordinarily you'd be willing to do that for her, wouldn't you?"

"Yes, Miss Toughclit. I would certainly help her out that way. If she wanted me to."

"Well because she's been naughty, I forbid you to do it to her. Now tell her you'd like to help her but I won't allow it because she's been so bad."

Glancing shyly at Gina, the man said, "Well, Little

Dripcunt, I know how much you like to get poked from behind. But I just can't help you. Miss Toughclit has forbidden it, and I have to do what she says. I'm sorry."

"Don't listen to her," Gina's player said. "You know you'd like it as much as me, wouldn't you? Can't you picture how good you'd feel?"

"Yes, but...."

"So ignore Miss Toughclit and get around in back of me and just slide it in. Please? Pretty please?"

"Don't you dare!" the mannequin ordered. "Remember, I'm in charge. Right?"

"Right, Miss Toughclit."

"Now pay attention. Another thing Little Dripcunt loves is getting sucked off. You like to do that to a woman, don't you?"

"Yes, Miss Toughclit."

"I bet you do. I'll bet you're pretty good at it, too, aren't you?"

"I guess I am. Miss Toughclit."

"Well, because Little Dripcunt's been such a tease, I don't want you doing that to her, either. Understand?"

"Yes, Miss Toughclit," he answered, blushing.

"I want you to tell her that as much as you'd like to

suck her off the way you know she likes a man to do, you just don't think she deserves it. So you're not going to give her the satisfaction."

The man took Gina by the arms and looked into her eyes purposefully before repeating the mannequin's message. Now she thought he looked more like Charles Lindberg, the aviator who had gotten Amelia Earhart into such a pickle. And so it went for the rest of the session: Miss Toughclit, the mannequin, would describe some position or form of foreplay that Little Dripcunt supposedly found tremendously exciting, only to demand that the customer explain to her that he just could not do that for her because she had been very naughty. Drips were mounting on the man's tip, and a quiver could be heard in his voice.

"Tell her this is what she gets for being such a tease," the mannequin's voice instructed. "Tell her she deserves this for leaving so many cocks twitching, unfulfilled."

"Oh, please, I'm gonna explode I'm so hot," Gina's player broadcast. "You can't keep me worked up like this! You gotta put it in and do me real good. Won't you please do that for me?"

The man longed to comply, but his excitement had built to a point where he could no longer control himself. He was talking to her, swimming in excitement and joy, holding her arms tightly and looking into the mirrors of passion he imagined in her eyes. Then he glanced down. She lowered her gaze as well, and they both saw his average-size, rock-hard, slightly bent penis go into spasms. Quivering like a multiple killer paying his debts to society in a souped-up electric chair, he pumped little bursts of coddle into the air six or seven times in a row.

When his spurts subsided, he was no longer able to look at her face. He wiped himself with a handful of tissues and then freed her hands. Unaware that the party was over, the mannequin continued its instructions—"tell Miss Dripcunt you're going to hold back until her begging is a little more believable"—until a freed Gina turned off its tape.

She was tempted to stick around for a little while to milk the unexpected advantage she had gained from his quick release, but she sensed it would be a violation of the spirit of their business. She stepped into the skirt she had put in her duffel, wanting to count the wad of bills she saw there but not daring to. She grabbed the mannequin under her arm and rejoined Tink, who ran forward to help her as soon as she opened the door.

Once she removed her false lips she began eulogizing the effectiveness of their new program. "You should've seen him!" she said. "He just went off! I didn't even have to touch him! The jerk just shot his wad into the air!"

Blushing and unable to look at her, Tink started the van and headed back to Midget's to get the next assignment.

She fell silent for a while but then turned philosophical. "I don't know if we should make this a regular part of our offering, though," she said.

He shot her a glance, but did not speak. He'd been working out extra hard on his stairmaster to improve his chances, and wondered if she had noticed his trimmer form.

"It just doesn't seem fair," she said. "Besides, it'd be pretty tough on the girls. I'm kind of frustrated, you know? I mean, all that excitement, and I didn't even get fucked. I'll bet someone with less experience wouldn't be able to take it. I'll tell you one thing, Tink, even for a pro like me, once a night's got to be the limit for a dry run like this. It just ain't natural!"

She was silent for a few blocks but then turned bitchy. "It's easy for Sammi to make these tapes and send us out. She never has to go on a visitation, not knowin' what to expect. I'm tempted to insist that she take a turn along with the rest of us so she has some idea of what we have to go through. Wouldn't that only be fair?"

Tink nodded.

"She don't give a shit about what we have to put up with. Sometimes I feel like just taking off. What do I need her for? I made it on my own before I met her and I could make it after. There's a big world out there and it's singing Welcome Gina!"

"We could do it," Tink said, his voice bubbling with a rich huskiness.

"Huh?"

"You an' me, Gina. We could take off, and go to some other town. I could work days. There's Radio Shack's everywhere. I could help you at night. We could do it, Gina."

She examined the doughy-muscled man for a full minute and then said, "I suppose we could, Tink. But let's not do anything hasty. Let's not say anything yet. We'll just bide our time, see how things play out." Falling silent, she cautioned herself to be more careful. 'This walrus is a sleeping volcano,' she thought. 'He could erupt at any moment.'

But her words were enough like a promise for him to take them to heart. A shudder ran through him. For the second time in less than an hour Gina's influence produced an unassisted, unintended spewing, followed by a protracted embarrassment. He could feel her looking at him, but maintained his silence. 'Jesus, he's like a priest who's heard his own confession,' she found herself thinking. 'He's probably telling himself he'd better be careful or this could get out of hand.'

But then the devil in her made her reach over and squeeze his thigh in a way she knew would stiffen him again.

It's what she did.

Chapter 12

Lieutenant Spezio and his lumbering shadow arrived in Toledo just after midnight. The first thing they did was cruise the central precinct's parking lot, hoping to spot the gold Blazer.

"There's probably a dozen outlying stations," Carpenter speculated.

"This guy would be here," Spezio informed him. "He'd be where the action is. Plus, this would be where Litwak sent Sherri's picture."

There were no gold Blazers in the parking lot.

"Well, let's find us a motel," Spezio said.

"I could drop you, and come back and stake out this place," Carpenter offered. "In case our guy shows up. Or Litwak."

"Litwak won't be here for two days. He's gotta be part of an operation tomorrow. I checked. He didn't cancel out. And I don't make our guy to be workin' the after-midnight shift. We'll get some sleep tonight and set up here tomorrow."

"What're you gonna do when we find him, boss?" Carpenter asked.

"I'm not sure. I'll know when I see him. If he's just a

weenie, I may squeeze him. But if he's a gamer, which is more likely, we'll have to find a different way to apply pressure. I brought my FBI badge, just in case. Nobody screws around with those guys."

"Except us," Carpenter observed, grinning.

The principals in the sex-tape business were celebrating in Midget's apartment: Midget, Tink, Sammi, Gina, and Rose. It was the end of their seventh week of successful operation. In honor of the occasion Sammi had stopped by the corner on 8th Street and bought them a $200 bag of coke and grabbed a case of Coors at a party store. She had forbidden Midget to steal anything more from downstairs. The store was frequently closed while the owner went from one clinic to another, hoping for a miracle.

Midget probably should have declined the coke since he was already buzzing along on a triple hit of speed, but passing something by just was not in his nature. Sammi noticed his accelerated volubility, though, and kept pushing beers at him in an attempt to hold him in check. He took one but only drank enough to wash down some oblong pills. She did not want to ask what they were.

"Too bad Alice took what happened personally," Rose remarked. She was wearing black pants, a bright orange top, and orange sandals, an outfit she had long wanted to buy for herself but had waited for until she had paid off Angel's braces.

"She's coming around," Sammi said. "I told her that

the woman she'd dated had called back, begging for another visit and saying she'd just been joking when she said Alice would have to pay. I asked Alice if she'd consider going back."

"Would she?" Gina asked.

"She's thinking it over. Like everything else, it'll probably come down to money."

"We really stumbled onto a bonanza," Rose remarked. "Who would've thought this little deal would be so rewarding."

"Speaking of that," Gina began. "I ran into Leona the other day. She finally saved up enough to get her new teeth."

"Does she take 'em out to go down on a guy?" Midget bubbled.

"I hope not," Gina said. "I knew a gal in Tallahassee who did that, and the guy grabbed 'em and pushed her out of the car. He wouldn't give 'em back unless she gave him all her dough. It sounded like a funny scene the way she described it. Her pounding on his window and gummin' her words. Screamin', 'If I does that, my man will break every bone in my body', and him insistin', 'what's it gonna be, your bones or your teeth?'"

"I heard about a girl who had a special set made out of foam rubber," Midget cackled.

"For guys like you, with a rubber dick," Sammi said.

"I'm glad Leona finally got 'em," Rose chirped. "They're gonna pay for themselves. You just wait and see. Nobody likes a girl with stink-mouth."

"Anyway, she said Tony's been lookin' for me. The guy who gave us our first script?"

"Oh ya," Rose said. "The google eyes."

"He's been drivin' back and forth by the railroad station. Askin' the girls where I'd moved to. I've had that effect on men my whole life."

"Anybody tell him?" Sammi asked.

"Nobody knows," Gina replied. "I've got half a mind to look him up and see what he wants. He wasn't as much of a jerk as most. Besides, we owe him for helping us get started."

Tink's complexion turned ashen. He did not like where this was going.

"Don't do it, Gina," Sammi warned. "Looking back is a dumb-shit move. It's like that song says. Don't make no dumb-shit move."

Midget was inspired to deliver a prediction: "You know what's gonna happen with this? People are getting hooked on it. There's something about the experience we provide that they can't get enough of. I'm telling you, we oughta think about upping our rates."

"We'd price ourselves out of work," Sammi declared.

"No way," Midget continued. "You just watch! We'll get a call from some jerk on his honeymoon. Sayin' he just can't get it up. Askin' us to send over a cassette player for his poor little wifey to wear."

"Oh sure," Rose countered.

"He's right," Tink put in. "The more people accept being told what to do, the more accustomed to it they become. It helps them avoid embarrassment. As long as they follow the directions on the tape, it isn't their fault if they screw up. Our tapes can help people get a life!"

When he stopped, there was a moment of silence during which the others looked at him, making him turn red. "Look at the way Russia was. Look at Cuba right now, for Christ's sake!"

Gina offered him more coke. When he declined she snorted the lines she had prepared for him. Seeing that, he protested, so she began chopping a new rock for him.

"I can see our tapes being used for therapy," Rose said. "Imagine that!"

"That's not too far-fetched of an idea," Sammi mused. "We ought to do a Therapy series."

"Would we be the doctor, or the patient?" Rose asked.

"Hmm. Maybe both."

"Hey, I still think we should sell ads on them!"

Midget announced, reaching for the fresh line that Gina had prepared for Tink.

"Huh?"

"Like, for Pepsi. You know, some guy's really getting it on, and here comes a little ten-second jingle about the Pepsi generation. What d'you think we could get for that?"

"P.O.O.B.. Put out of business," Sammi intoned.

"Or subliminal messages," Midget went on, effortlessly shifting gears. "Hey, Tink, let's try dubbing a voice that can't quite be heard and see what happens. We'll have it say, 'Call Jimmy Wainwrite, he runs the best girls in town'. Okay?"

"You don't run me," Rose said.

They all laughed. Looking around, Gina felt they had become a kind of family. It was a special moment. Ordinarily the first intimation of a feeling like this made her uneasy, but this time she was able to accept it. Apparently something had changed.

"Hey, I know, let me do twins," Gina said, catching a new drift out of the blue. "I'll wear two tapes, and play both parts."

"How?" Rose wondered.

"With my eyes, my posture. I can do it!"

"She might have a point," Sammi thought. "We could

collect double."

"The two tapes would have to be synchronized," Rose pointed out.

"That's what we do anyway," Tink declared. But why did it always have to be Gina?

"I had a call from Aberdeen," Midget said. Rose tittered; Aberdeen was the locus of and synonym for Toledo's community of queers. "A guy named Donald Farrington asked if we could send him a boy."

"Did you tell him you'd be right over?" Gina joked.

"Hell fucking no!"

"I hope you wrote down the number," Sammi said. "There's no tellin' how far we'll branch out. There could be a lot of money in somethin' like that, and I personally think it'd be good to cover as many bases as we can."

"Hey, if a guy don't pay?" Rose said. "We can wrap him up and send him out! Seeing what we have to put up with'll make him a little more understanding, eh?"

On a roll, Midget had yet another idea: "Here's something I'm getting a lot of calls for. A tape where a woman tells her lover that she really needs him so she can forget about her stupid husband who doesn't know the first thing about making her come. You'd be surprised how many guys wanna hear that from a girl."

This hit a little too close to home for Gina so she

changed the subject. "Remember how this got started?" she asked. "That guy who hired me was trying to get back at his friend. It was a set-up. Once his friend got used to girls showing up with a tape player on, you know, he was gonna kidnap some woman at the mall and send her up to his buddy's door with a tape. His buddy would think she was just pretending and give her everything he had. When he set her free the splut would really hit the fan."

"That's sick," Rose declared, wrinkling her nose. "Sick sick sick," she giggled.

"I told you he wasn't so bad!" Gina chirped.

"Who can say how the straight bitch would react," Sammi mused. "What if she liked it? Maybe it would change her life. Maybe she'd just leave without making a fuss. Maybe she'd go back on her own, as soon as she could. Maybe she would become our best customer for buying tapes. Maybe she'd strap on every one of them and when she was done start over again."

"I know!" Midget burst in. "Let's do a tape for First Communion! 'Take, eat, this is my body!' That'd be one way to bring Alice back into the fold."

"I was raised a Catholic," Rose coldly interjected. On that note, silence descended with a thud. The festive atmosphere evaporated, and everyone knew the party was over.

The next morning, Wednesday, a freshly-waxed gold

Blazer was in the lot when Spezio and Carpenter arrived. They jimmied the door and got the owner's name from the registration, and went inside and asked for Pete Garitty.

The overweight cop at the desk directed them upstairs, where Pete was sitting on a table in a room with a half dozen other vice cops listening to stories of what the previous evening had brought. All of them were adept at using the mundane events of what had actually happened as jumping-off points for their lurid personal fantasies. Nobody believed anybody else, but this regular morning session had more appeal than most TV shows.

Spezio beckoned him into the hall and asked if there were somewhere they could talk. Garitty led them to his office, a typical cramped cranny but with two windows, thanks to its corner location. The scruffed old desk was overflowing with paperwork, just like every cop's desk Spezio had ever seen, including his own.

Spezio decided to go with the FBI bit. He showed Garitty a badge identifying him as Ralph Wonderly out of Cleveland—a friend of his there had helped him set it up. Any queries would produce the response, 'He's on special assignment. That's all we can say.'

"What's this about?" Pete wanted to know.

"We're after a bad cop," Spezio told him.

"Can't help you. Don't know any."

"He's in Detroit," Spezio threw out, watching Pete's eyes closely.

"Oh?"

"He's headed here to eliminate his girlfriend. He thinks she knows too much. He made the mistake of blabbing about his deals to impress her. Pillow talk, you know. She took off on him and he's been worried sick that she's gonna rat him out. Thing is, she doesn't know squat. We've talked to her. She doesn't have enough to build a case around. That's why we couldn't put her in Witness Protection. Our best shot is to catch him in the act of tryin' to snuff her."

"What's this got to do with me?" Pete asked, lighting up a cigarette despite his constant hack. Just one more couldn't make a difference.

"We understand you contacted him," Spezio said. Carpenter stood to the side with his arms folded across his chest, exuding menace. It was his specialty.

"Oh?"

"He sent pictures of her to every precinct in the Midwest, claiming she was his wife. He's trading on his position as a cop, which we don't appreciate. Anyway, you told him you had a line on her. He offered you, what, a thousand bucks?"

"Twelve hundred," Pete replied.

Spezio breathed more easily upon hearing this.

Getting a straight answer meant the Toledo vice cop had bought his act. "Between you and me," Spezio said. "That's an insult. The prick's loaded. What d'you think, Ed," he added, glancing at Carpenter, "he's got at least a quarter million in cash lying around, right?"

Carpenter nodded, daydreaming about the handsomely stout waitress who had served him breakfast. He was sure their momentary eye contact had not been an accident. Maybe when this job was done....

"Personally, as we let this thing play out, I'd like to see you lighten him up a little more than a fuckin' measly twelve hundred. A slimebag like Litwak don't deserve to have a retirement fund, know what I mean?"

Pete nodded; these guys were talking his language. "What d'you want me to do?"

"First, have you got the dame stashed, or is she still on the street?"

"She's still walkin' around, but we're watching for her. She's part of some kinky new scheme involving bondage. And taped instructions for the johns. It's a fad right now. We're just getting a handle on who all the players are before we close 'em down."

"That sounds like Sherri, eh, Ed?"

Carpenter grunted.

"She's using a different name here," Pete told them. "Gina."

"She was Lola in Atlanta. She never stays in one place very long. How does she get her customers?"

"They're placing ads in the sex columns of the local papers."

"Where's their base?"

"We haven't been able to track it. They've got some kind of scrambler on the phone line they use."

"Shit, I ought to call the office and have them send you our latest piece of equipment. We got a guy in Phoenix with it who was bouncing his calls all over the world with some kind of computer deal. He had seven different relays set up, each one with a secret access code. We busted through all of them and wound up sittin' outside his door."

Pete exhaled to express his awe. "So what d'you want me to do?"

"Litwak will be here tomorrow," Spezio began.

"Here?"

"Right here. When he makes contact, don't act surprised. Don't give him any leverage. Play him for all he's worth, and keep us informed. Okay? We're at the Ottawa Motel. Room 12."

"I don't suppose there's any bonus money you could spread around," Pete asked. "I mean, I'll be at risk here."

"No, but you'll have our enduring gratitude," Spezio

told him. He had learned the hard way not to promise more than he had to.

Both men shook Garitty's hand before they left, with Carpenter almost breaking it. That was his little trick for not being taken for granted. Walking down the street to where they had parked, Spezio asked his sidekick how he had done.

"Fine," Carpenter said. "Except you know I hate being a fuckin' Ed. Can't you call me Sam or Bill? I knew an Ed where I grew up and he was the dumbest shithead in the neighborhood. I thought I'd left him behind when I hit the road for D-ville."

Once they were in Spezio's Gran Prix Carpenter asked what they were going to do.

"Nothing," Spezio answered, smiling. "Our friend Litwak's going to shoot his wife in a jealous rage over her turning tricks. Then Pete Garitty's gonna shoot Litwak. Pete will wind up with a commendation."

"So how do we get started doin' this nothin'?"

"We get us a paper and begin orderin' up whores until Sherri comes knock-knock-knockin' on our door. We might have to go through a half dozen before we find her, though. You up for that?"

"All in the line of duty," the big man grunted.

Being out of town, Spezio had not heard the news: around midnight, Big Daddy Do, the former James

Arthur Dooley Junior, accidentally blew his brains out in his girlfriend's apartment in St. Claire Shores on Detroit's north side. He had beaten her up again in a crack frenzy and was laughing and pointing his gun around the room. According to the bimbo, he had asked her, 'What'm I supposed to do, feel so sorry that I'll shoot myself?' He had pointed the gun at his head and had started coughing, and it just went off. Well, with a little shove.

Gus Litwak received a phone call from Vito, one of the cops on the graveyard shift, telling him Big Daddy had iced himself so the stakeout was off. "Personally, I think the broad shot him," Vito said. "I told her, If I let you skate on this you're gonna owe me big time. Maybe you can help me collect, Gus. She's got enough puss for the whole damn squad."

Gus did not have to think about what to do. He grabbed his suitcase, jumped in his Mercury Cougar, and drove to Toledo in fifty-seven minutes. He didn't really have a plan. All he knew for sure was that getting closer to Sherri was a whole lot better than going back to bed and lying there, dreading hearing the blissful bluebirds and robins outside the window announce that it was time to get up and begin another miserable day.

By 2:15 he had located the central precinct, where he had mailed the picture of his wife. There wasn't much action. He sat there for twenty minutes and then drove to a hotel a few blocks away, asking for a wake-up call for 7:00.

When he finally got to sleep he had one of the dreams that were becoming more frequent, of the time before his first wife had left. In it, he and Marge had won a house in some promotion, and drove out to see what it was like. It reminded him of the many Naval Base homes his mother had moved them into in the vagabond junket of his childhood.

He and Marge stood outside a short white fence in gleaming sunshine, looking at the tidy bungalow. She had slimmed down and died her hair blonde. When he turned to say something he discovered she had already gone into the back yard. He found her down on her hands and knees in the garden, pruning some flowers. "Why would anybody give this house away?" she remarked. "Look how good the soil is! I just planted these petunias a few minutes ago, and they're already in bloom."

Suddenly he was afraid of what she was about to say. He waved his hands to forestall her but she just blurted it out: "Just like little Joey."

He knew what would happen. Sure enough, before his eyes the flowers developed desiccated leaves and withered stalks. The pedals turned black and blew away in the breeze, but she did not notice. Dreading what he knew he had to do, he opened his mouth, hoping that this time he would find the right words to tell her about Joey, that he had only been a figment of their imagination. But the phone rang, waking him, saving him.

Drenched in sweat, it took him three cups of coffee to

shake off his dream. He'd had it before, in one form or another, and he had no idea what it could mean.

After showering, he drove back to the police station. He was more unsettled than usual, and felt out of synch. Unsure of what to do next, he parked across the street and waited for his head to clear. He started thinking about Margaret Stormhauser, and how she was more complicated and interesting than he had given her credit for. Perhaps when this was over he would take a week off and they would go on a trip. Maybe to Yellowstone, or Vegas. If he did okay at the craps table he might take her to see the Mormon Tabernacle Choir.

His reveries dissolved when Spezio and his oafish shadow came striding self-confidently down the broad granite steps. Spezio's stagger filled Gus with rage. It was as if the arrogant rooster were telling the world that he had screwed Gus's wife and was proud of it. Gus had to fight the urge to run them down, which he was only able to do by reminding himself how good he would feel when Spezio was arrested for the Vandelay murder.

He followed them at a safe distance. He pulled over when they stopped at a newsstand, and then tailed them to the Ottawa Motel and watched them go into #12. Then he parked in the used car lot across the street, positioning himself so he could see their door. When one of the salesmen came over to speak to him he flashed his badge and told him not to pay any attention to him. He wouldn't be there any longer than he had to.

The one thing Gus was sure of was that Spezio was

not there for a tryst with Sherri. Not if the Carp was along. He was a throwback to the Age of the Goons, a Neanderthal, where women were concerned, who could not control himself in their presence. At the police station they'd had to pass a rule to keep him away from the caged whores. A couple of the girls had talked about pressing charges—which would have ruined this fringe benefit for everyone. The number of new recruits would drop off the table. Carpenter's brutality would have gotten him kicked off the force long ago if Spezio had not found him handy.

The fact that Spezio was there with Carpenter did not bode well for Sherri, Gus thought. The Carp's presence changed things. Now he should only observe. Whatever happened would happen. It was not his place to interfere—just as it had not been at the Bull's Balls when he had watched as Terkel had tried to cut his wife almost a full year ago. Sherri always acted like she understood how things were, he thought. Well, she should have learned that there could be a dangerous side to that life.

If Spezio had the Carp cancel Sherri's subscription to Life, Gus would have to take the big man in. Everyone would know he had acted on Spezio's orders, and would offer him the moon to get him to flip. However it turned out, it would make it more difficult for Spezio to dodge the Vandelay rap.

Sitting in the Mormon Tabernacle, whatever the hell that was, Marge would never guess why he would have such a big smile.

Chapter 13

Wednesday was a busy day for Midget. He woke up at noon, heavy-eyed and fog-headed, as was usual lately. Sure somebody was messing with his shit, he fought his way out of the dirty blankets in which he had entangled himself and took a hit to clear his mind.

This time it back-fired. For ten minutes he could not remember who or where he was. His mind went completely blank. Sick with panic, he crouched over the toilet and discharged the remains of buffalo wings and a pineapple pizza. Eventually it started coming back, one mirage-like detail at a time. He took another hit so he wouldn't forget.

By 12:45 he was stable enough to check his messages. A half dozen calls had come in requesting visitations and another dozen asking to purchase cassettes. Someone had called twice to ask if they had a tape called, You Be the Sheep. His first reaction was to assume it was a prank, but when he thought about it he was not so sure. With his third hit it became his own wonderful notion—yet another Wainwrite brainstorm.

It was going to be a busy day. Poppy was supposed to make a tape for the Aberdeen customers before she went on her first call. Sammi intended to show up a little later to make one for their Moving to Melrose series. There were so many calls coming in that he could not check their new clients as thoroughly as he would have liked.

Gina arrived about 1:00. Midget held out a slip for the Ottawa Motel. "A new customer," he told her. "He didn't have anything particular in mind so I just grabbed a tape off the pile."

"I don't like motel calls," Gina said. "What else you got?"

"This guy's pretty damn horny. He left three messages and when I called him back he said he'd pay double for quick service."

Midget tried to hand it to her again, but she turned away. "C'mon, it's good dough," Midget whined.

"She don't want to take it," Tink said, awkwardly forceful. "Give her something else."

Midget did, but he did not like the way Tink had become so protective of her. He was shadowing her more than ever these days, waiting for chances to do her favors. To get back at her for having commandeered his friend's attention, Midget gave her a slip he had earmarked for Leona for an appointment in Waterville, out Highway 23.

Tink took it, as her driver. "Jesus, Midget, this is an extra 45 minutes each way!"

"Sammi wants us to work the boonies, spread out the operation," Midget replied. "What can I say?"

"That's okay," Gina told him. "Let's go." She was counting points against Midget, and this insult put him over a hundred. She did not know how she'd get him back but was certain she would. 'Maybe I'll ask Sammi about making Midget go on a call,' she thought, angrily eyeing the little man. 'He's getting too bossy. Besides, I'll bet he'd look good in a wig.'

"Aren't you gonna suit up?" Midget asked.

"In Tink's van," Gina told him. "I know you wanna watch, but you'll just have to use your imagination. As usual."

Poppy was arriving as Gina and Tink left. They chatted briefly on the stairs. "I see he's closed again downstairs," Poppy remarked.

"The guy probably won't make it. If he cacks I'll clean him out, and then we'll have a party. So what's up today?"

"I gotta make a tape for Aberdeen," Poppy confided, rolling her eyes. "Then I'm gonna visit a little nerd in Perrysburg who thinks a voice is gonna ask him nicely to kiss my ass. All I can say is, he's in for one hell of a surprise."

"Good luck."

Inside, Midget had just received a fourth call from the Ottawa Motel. "Hey, Poppy, wanna make some big bucks doin' a quick one? This guy can't wait any longer."

"Sorry, can't," she told him. "Sammi wants me to tape her new script for the Aberdeen crowd. So she can listen to it and modify it when she gets here. Then I'm off to Perrysburg. What about Rose?"

"Her daughter's in a class play for the 9th graders so she's got the day off. Get this, the girl is playing a fuckin' nun!"

"What's wrong with that? I think we're all nuns, in a sense. We've got to wear our special robes, and repeat the same old things that nobody could possibly believe but everybody pretends to. And no matter what we start out goin' after, we all wind up denying ourselves in the end. By the time we get what we're after it's lost its appeal."

"Maybe I can get Leona to come in," Midget thought out loud. "She's scheduled for after supper anyway." To do her reading Poppy went into the living room, where Tink had set up their recording studio. The exercise bike had disappeared but the gas barbecue had not yet found a new owner. And the fruits of Midget's increasingly chaotic hepped-up shopping sprees cluttered the room. The only worthwhile purchase had been a thousand dollar sewing machine, to which Tink had taken like a fish to water; he had started making their costumes, and had surprised the gang with his proficiency. His tiny hands flew over the myriad buttons, selecting stitch styles and spacing with confident aplomb.

Midget phoned Leona, his jittery fingers getting it right on the third try. 'God damn,' he told himself. 'This fuckin' speed's getting weaker every time. Time for a little more. Or maybe it was yesterday that I had the last hit and I'm just misremembering.'

Leona was still asleep, but she regarded herself as a good trouper. She said she would be ready to go by the time someone picked her up. She had her costume, and the tape she had used in her last assignment the night before.

"Which one?" Midget asked.

"You've had Naughty Thoughts About Me, Son. The only thing is, it's hard for me to be a mother. I'm too young."

"Right. That one's okay. Oh, shit!" Midget said. "I forgot. Pomi's studying for his mid-terms. Oh well, if he won't do it I suppose I can do it myself. It'll be good to get away from the God-damn phones for awhile. They've been ringing off the hook. Okay, one of us'll be there in half an hour."

But the always-agreeable Pomi said he would pick up Leona and take her to the Ottawa. He thought he could study in his car while he waited for her. "Perhaps these obstinate formulas will become more compliant in the open air."

"Call me when you're done," Midget said. "The way the day's going, we might have to dispatch you from there. So bring plenty of books."

"You pay extra for all this hectic run-around, eh, boss?"

"You bet, Pomi"—thinking happily, 'I know who I can get to mix up something for the little jerk, scramble him a little, make him easier to handle.'

Sammi rose early that same Wednesday morning in order to make breakfast for her husband Stanley, as she did every day. To be companionable she ate a little camembert on wheat thins with him and asked him what his morning held. She had always prided herself on being good at talking to older men. At letting her eyes imply she was listening and cared while her head took a tour of other worlds.

He was in for a grueling encounter, he told her. TKD, of which he was vice-president, had become a potential victim for some corporate raiders from Pennsylvania. He had to plan his strategy carefully. If TKD was bought out by the wrong group, all the executives would immediately lose their jobs. His pension would be in danger—that fund was a target for the vultures who were drooling over the possibility of plying their tricks to pick it clean. Now, if he could just scare these Pittsburgh guys off, and give Louie Garafolo a chance.... Stanley had found Sweet Lou muy simpatico; they had really hit it off.

As well as being a good talker, Sammi was a good listener. She felt this enabled her to make an occasional helpful suggestion. For his part Stanley treasured her intelligence as much as her glamour. He had never regretted divorcing his wife of 22 years in order to marry her. That busybody had alluded to Sammi's questionable past, but he had told her he did not care what she had been. He loved her for who she was now. Sammi knew better than to confess unnecessarily; she had friends who had, and they were all sorry afterwards. Besides, by not being told the specific details, he was able to fantasize every imaginable possibility during their passionate Saturday-night sessions.

This morning he reminded her that his son would be driving there from Cleveland for dinner. The boy was a student at CSU, and Stanley guessed he wanted his permission to change his major again. Sammi suggested tolerance. In her opinion, any education was infinitely better than none, so whichever way it went there would not be any loser.

She liked the boy. He was still on his mother's side, but Sammi had an idea how she could win him over as soon as she had some free time. She was looking forward to it; the sad-eyed, droop-shouldered kid was really just an overgrown puppy, and would be as easy to train. She had been born with a carrot, which she enjoyed alternating with a stick. Maybe then he could introduce her new business to the fraternity crowd.

They kissed at the door, and she watched Stanley get in his Lincoln to drive to the plant. Then she went into her bedroom, tossed off a shot of scotch, and set her alarm for 2:00 in the afternoon. After putting on her blinders she climbed into bed.

It seemed like only a moment later when the alarm went off. She awoke in a daze, reached for her bottle of bennies, and swallowed three as she stumbled toward the shower. By the time the room had filled with steam she was pretty much back to being her normal self.

She stood in the shower letting the water riddle her back. At times like this it was better than any man. She thought through some of the lines she'd written for her Welcome to Melrose tape: 'I just arrived here from the midwest, and I'd give anything if you'd let me move into the empty apartment. I know whoever moves in will be joining a kind of family, and you only want the right person, but I really believe I can convince you that's me.' She would weave in some facts from some of the episodes being rerun on cable to make it more believable.

The script was getting closer, she thought. She had taped a few segments of the show and watched them closely to get the actors' inflections down better. She knew she could sound like Heather Locklear. She had a real talent for voices because she could hear them talking in her head. More and more she realized she was only a vehicle for greater forces. It was funny how she was getting smaller and larger at the same time.

This tape was particularly important to her because she hoped it would lead to a whole new market of visitations based on TV shows. Baywatch would be next, and then perhaps Dr. Quinn. Was that still on? She had an idea for Jayne Seymour as the Joyce Brothers of the wild west. That smile of Seymour's always seemed to be taunting someone about sex. She only wished she could be there when the actress finally got what she had been asking for.

'Poppy can do Ellen,' she thought, turning off the water. 'She'll be really good.' She felt so light and feathery that she grabbed another two bennies for good measure. As far as she was concerned, it was a wonderful day.

Across town Tony was worried that Jake Plummer was getting close to finding Gina. Bob and Ray had started acting smug at the plant, as if they knew something. When he followed them to Studs the week before and tried to draw Bob out after Ray and the others left, Bob clammed up. It pained Tony that after he had lowered himself to Bob's level he had been rebuffed.

Tony was surprised how much Gina's plight was bothering him. How much she was on his mind. For weeks he had been cruising various seamy neighborhoods, hoping to find her new location. He had not been able to stop thinking about her, although he would not admit that his obsession was more than a desire to warn her of the cops closing in. Even though she had abandoned him, he felt responsible for her fate. He had gotten her into this, and he had to do something to help.

Worried that he would get picked up on a surveillance camera, his cruises were like races: at or over the speed limit, with quick glances out of the corner of his eye. He was beginning to feel Gina must have left town. The idea was both reassuring and saddening. If she had, she wouldn't be arrested. Plus, none of the guys at the plant would ever know of his involvement in Bob's encounter. But that would also mean he had lost the chance of something developing between the two scofflaws.

In the early afternoon his gasket-maker at the factory threw a rod. The maintenance crew promised to have it running by Thursday morning but the rest of Wednesday was shot. He announced that he expected to be paid for the lost hours. After all, it was not his fault that the equipment had broken down.

To not get in the way, he offered to take off. That was okay with everyone. In an aside to the coke-bottle-eyed Arnie, Ray said, "Hey, get someone to pick up Tony's machine with a fork lift and dump it in the trash. Then maybe we'll be rid of the jerk-off, once and for all."

Tony looped past the old train station on his way home, wondering if Gina might have just changed shifts. It was not likely. Most of the girls, probably 85, 90%, preferred working at night, when the darkness facilitated their disguise. But there was Trixie, standing in front of a bankrupt camera store with its faded 'Going Out Of Business' signs still dangling from fatigued tape in the sunny storefront window. He had known her a year ago, but then she had disappeared.

He pulled over, parked down the street, and walked back to chat with her for old time's sake. She remembered him as well, not in detail, but without any cautioning red flags. So she asked him how things were going.

"Good. Good. Where've you been?"

"Hospital," she told him. "I got my appendix cut out, but there was a complication. I was laid up almost two months. I'm still too weak to work nights. I got me a lawyer, though, and he's gonna sue their sorry asses for what they done. I coulda died!"

They talked for awhile before Tony asked her if she knew Gina.

"She your new squeeze?" she asked.

"When I gave her a ride she left an earring in my car."

"What kinda ride, big boy?"

"I just want to give it back. Know where she hangs out?"

"Give it to me and I'll see that she gets it."

"You gonna give me my reward too?"

She looked at him for a minute before she had not seen much of Gina lately, but that Alice, one of the waitresses at Wendell's, might know where she was.

It was worth a shot. He did not have anything else to do so he drove over to the old-fashioned restaurant. It was five after three when he sat down at the counter.

The place struck him as a real throwback. A weak pastel lime green ceiling and beige walls. Leatherette cushions on the stools surrounding the double camel-hump white counter. Heavy wooden doors leading to the bathrooms. He guessed the juke box offered all the hits of the 1950s.

The horsy waitress who brought him coffee made his quest easy: her name was sewn on her blouse. He felt jittery seeing it, and tried to make a little small talk to calm himself.

She listened to him because there were only two other customers at that off-hour. But she soon drifted toward the other end of the counter; something about him made her hackles rise. Failing to engage her made him even more anxious. The only thing working in his favor was that she was somewhat homely; the more attractive a woman was, the more difficulty Tony had in speaking to her. Yet she was wearing her new Jesus-fish ring, which swung her back in the other direction. For a moment he wondered if he should go somewhere and buy a Bible before trying to engage her in conversation.

The next time she passed by he ordered an egg-salad sandwich. When she brought it over he was seized with an inspiration and tried a different line. "I sure hope the developers get their plan approved," he remarked. "It would be good for business."

"What developers?" she wondered. "What plan?"

"The Garafalos," he said, making it up as he went. "They want to rehab the train station."

"Oh really? I hadn't heard about that."

"My cousin works for the Mayor. Not doing anything important, just arranging his dinners and parties. He has to make sure the prayer is appropriate," he threw in. "Sometimes he hears things, you know? These guys want to put shops on the first floor, and apartments up above. I guess there's plenty of room for parking where the tracks used to be."

"Is it still gonna look like a train station? We lived by the tracks when I grew up and didn't need no alarm clock because the 7-0-3 was always on time."

"As much as possible. They know it's important to preserve our heritage. I mean, that's who we are, right? They want to change it as little as they have to on the outside."

"When is this supposed to take place? Probably not til after I'm dead and gone, with my luck. Oh well...."

"No, as soon as they get all the permits," he told her. "Don't tell anyone. Obtaining the permits is a delicate proposition. It's harder than arranging financing, or actually doing the work. Maybe I shouldn't have said anything, but you look like someone I can trust."

"Thanks," she told him.

An elderly couple came in and sat down, and Alice went over to them with menus and glasses of water. When she passed Tony again, he asked, "Say, where's Gina been? I haven't seen her around for a couple of weeks."

"Probably over at Midget's," Alice answered. "She's too good for us now."

"He still live at the same place?"

"Yeah, up above Preston's Party Store. I hear it's going out of business. That's okay by me. Old Man Preston's been mean to me ever since I was a little girl."

Bingo! He got up to go. Abandoning the barely-touched sandwich, he peeled off all his ones—six of them—and left her a generous tip.

Chapter 14

Pomi deposited Leona at the Ottawa Motel at 2:45. He parked in the lot where he had a view of the door, and dialed the customer on the cell phone Midget had provided. When his call was answered, he pushed the play button on his tape player, and a sultry voice informed the customer that someone delightfully exciting was waiting outside the door.

Then Pomi opened his textbook and tried to memorize the formulas governing deflection in steel beams. But the terms swam in front of his eyes. It was next to impossible to make any sense of them. On the verge of tears, he cursed himself again for lacking the courage to tell his family that he did not want to be an engineer. What he really wanted was to work in a hospital. Even as just an orderly. Perhaps someday go to medical school to become an emergency room physician. That was what he had a talent for: helping out in a time of crisis. But how could he ever make his father understand? The old autocrat would never even listen.

Pomi could not even entertain the notion of just doing what he wanted in defiance of his father's wishes. What he needed was a special tape in a player strapped to his head chanting Be your own man. Just do it.

From across the street Spezio snapped some pictures, just in case. He was a creature of habit, and this was standard procedure. Examining Leona through his binoculars made him chuckle. Despite her make-up and wig, he'd had enough experience gauging women to see that she was definitely past her prime. It reaffirmed his choice of letting the Carp have her so he could follow her when she left; his helper would not object to over-ripe fruit but he sure as hell would. His standards were higher. Once they had fixed Litwak and pulled off a few last big jobs, it would be nothing but the best for him.

He had told Carpenter that if it was not Sherri he should fuck her quickly, ask her if she could call to have Sherri sent over because he had a huge appetite, and then, either way, let her leave so he could follow her back to her base. He had asked the big man not to waste any time. "Fifteen minutes should be all you need, right?" he had asked.

"That don't give me time to do much," the Carp had replied.

"This's business, not pleasure. After we've done what we came for we'll get us some top grade poon tang. I know of a new place you're really gonna love," he promised. "If you think sideways is a hot slit, wait'll you try diagonal."

"Huh?"

"You'll see. Trust me on this." He did not have anything particular in mind, but figured he could always find something when he needed. He had a nose for this kind of thing.

Fifteen minutes turned into 20, and then 25. Spezio was fuming. Once again he asked himself why he had saddled himself with a dunderhead who could not even follow a simple command. 'I'll be damned if he gets a full share,' he told himself, hardly for the first time.

When his watch indicated it had been a half hour, Spezio decided to call the room to remind Carpenter of his instructions. He was just convincing himself that the call could give his idiot cohort an excuse to let the woman go. 'Something's come up,' he could say. But then the door to #12 opened and the Carp appeared, half in, half out. Standing in his undershirt and boxer shorts with his signature stupid grin, he motioned for Spezio to come over.

Pomi saw him as well. And Spezio, receiving the signal. Realizing that something was wrong, Pomi started his car, backed hurriedly around, and headed for the street. Spezio debated whether or not to follow him. He decided to, but the Carp motioned more frantically so he let Pomi go. He could always get Garitty to run the plate and chase him down later.

Inside, Leona was lying on the bed, in bad shape. Her gaudy false lips had been roughly ripped off, and her face was a pulpy mess. She was half murmuring, half sobbing, and there was a broad smear of blood on her thigh.

"What the hell happened?" Spezio demanded.

"She wouldn't tell me where to find Sherri," the Carp

explained in a voice implying that this was not his fault.

"Jesus H. Christ!" Spezio raged. "You God-damned idiot!"

"What'd I do? You said to ask her where Sherri was before I let her go. I asked, but she wouldn't tell."

Having no choice but to make the best of it, Spezio slapped Leona's cheeks until she was conscious and then told her, in his most paternal voice, that she needed help and they would get it for her, but first she had to tell them where to find Sherri.

"I don't know any Sherri," she got out, one eye still closed from an expanding bruise.

"She's probably going by a different name," Spezio coaxed.

"Ask Midget," she moaned. "He's the dispatcher."

"Where can we find Midget?"

"Above Preston's. On 4th Street," she murmured.

Feeling triumphant, Spezio turned to the Carp and gloated that it was just a matter of knowing how to talk to a woman. That was all that most of life boiled down to, Spezio felt.

The Carp was impressed. "What now, boss?" he asked.

"What d'you think? I'll back the car up to the door so

we can put her in the trunk. The local cops know we're staying here, so we can't leave her."

Sensing what they intended, Leona began to cry. "I just got new teeth," she wailed. "They cost me over five fucking grand. Have a heart."

"Shut her the fuck up," Spezio ordered in disgust, going for their car.

The two men headed for 4th street with Leona's body in the trunk. They felt it would be safer to take it back to Detroit to dump it, where they knew plenty of places. Some were getting full—yet there were more thugs than ever in D-ville.

"Hey, I got an idea," Spezio said.

"What's that, boss?"

"After we take care of Litwak, let's put the broad in his bed. In his apartment on Dequindre. That'll sidetrack any investigation those assholes want to start."

"Boss, you're a genius."

Midget's place was twenty minutes away. Spezio was a little worried that the Paki who skedadled would warn them, but there was nothing he could do about that now. If whoever was running the operation closed it and moved out, they would just have to track them down. It would not be hard. They'd grab the Paki and force him to talk. Squeezing the little brownie might be kind of fun. Spezio thought he might even do more than watch.

They needn't have worried—at least not about Pomi. When he saw that an obvious cop had been staking out Leona's assignment, it confirmed his growing fear: nothing good for him ever lasted. It gave him a chance to break with his stupid life, and he took it: he drove to his apartment, loaded everything into his station wagon, stopped at the bank to withdraw his $3700 savings, and was on the road to Lexington Kentucky before five. He had secretly looked in the phone book, and had seen that there were several hospitals and clinics there. When they saw his sincerity one of them would surely give him a job. Then he would write to his father. But not right away. So he did not need a strap-on command center to stand up and be a man.

Spezio and the Carp had nothing to worry about from Pomi, but Sammi's husband Stanley was a different matter. He had not gotten to where he was by playing a fool, and he was sure something was going on. The signs had been mounting for weeks.

He was acutely aware of the differences between his beautiful young wife and himself, and had no illusions about why she had married him. Naturally he expected certain things from her in exchange for what he provided, the freedom for her to pretend to be the person she'd always dreamed of. Not necessarily faithfulness. He could tolerate an occasional affair as long as it remained subsidiary to the main thrust of their relationship. But he demanded she behave conscientiously. He did not want to look ridiculous in the eyes of his friends.

Ten days ago or so he had begun to wonder what was going on. She seemed to only be going through the motions on their Saturday night rendezvous, as though other things of greater importance were happening in her life. Sometimes she was too distracted to keep up her end of their preliminary acting-out, which for him was necessary foreplay. She was becoming careless as well; she had forgotten their dinner engagement with Bunny and Lou Garafolo. Didn't she know how important that had been to him? If he could close that deal, if he could get Louie to buy into TKD based on the books he'd cooked up ... well, maybe what his attorney had suggested was right on, that when he headed out for a tropical paradise with no extradition it would be time to find a new and younger girl. He was extremely disappointed because he had thought Sammi would be a real asset in impressing Lou and disrupting his attention. From the way Lou talked, it was obvious what he liked.

Last Saturday night when she was taking a shower after they made love, which had been a real strain because she had gotten her lines out of sequence, he had done a quick search of her room and had found all that money. Actually it had not been much more than $7,000, but in cash it had looked like a larger amount. In a sense it was worse than finding a love letter. It bespoke of crime, of harmful secrets, and, ultimately, of betrayal.

A few days ago Stanley had pretended to sleep but had taken some no-doze so he could lie there without drifting off. He thought he should get an Oscar for the quality of his phony snores. Sometime after midnight his wife had gotten up, dressed in a sheer, tight pantsuit, and left the house. He had jumped out of bed and tried to follow her but he'd had to stay back because of his headlights, and he lost her somewhere downtown.

On Tuesday he gave her a repair kit to put in her trunk containing a small transmitter that he could follow—it had cost $1800 and he'd threatened to punch the seller in the nose if it didn't work. He was not worried that she'd find it—she was not the type to ever use a tool, except in the bedroom. Today he had gone to work but had come back after lunch and was sitting around the corner in his silver Lexus watching an LED screen. He had mixed emotions—both excitement and despair—when it indicated she was on the move.

She seemed lost in thought, sometimes driving too fast, sometimes too slow. Twice he almost caught up to her without intending to and had to turn off and then loop back to follow at a safer distance. He came upon her again just after she'd parked her Viper and was walking up the rickety steps to a dumpy apartment above a closed convenience store; he could watch her from behind for the rest of his life.

It was 3:18, according to the Rolex which had been a gift from his first wife on the occasion of their 20th anniversary. He had gotten over his guilt rather quickly; after all, he had made the money. She'd had a good ride. He just hoped he would someday get his son to agree.

He parked down the street and walked back. It was an unsavory neighborhood, and he was glad he had brought his Colt, just in case.

He stopped at the bottom of the steps and looked around. There was nobody to be seen, but his heart was pumping wildly anyway. He told himself he would have to get Dr. Jenkins to increase his medication—it was about time the quack with his greased mustache earned his retainer by prescribing more than the latest experimental Viagra. All of the excitement was getting to be too much for him.

He stepped onto the cobbled-up stairs. When they noticeably creaked he froze in his tracks. Five minutes went by before he dared take another step. When the second tread groaned more loudly than the first he froze again. He noticed his hand on the railing had developed an uncontrollable tremble.

Inside, Sammi could not get into her Melrose script. She sat in the studio room for a few minutes, fiddling with her tie and trying to get into the right mood but was just too jittery. Maybe she had grabbed more bennies than she had thought, she remarked to Midget when she got up and joined him in the kitchen.

"You need a lude," Midget told her.

"No thanks," she said, glancing around the filthy room. 'We should get out of this dump,' she told herself. 'Set up in a better pad. This place stinks. It gives me the creeps.'

"They're quick-acting, great for counteracting buzz,"

he said. "They make you feel dreamy. All the other great actresses take 'em with their Cheerios."

She felt he wanted her to ask him what a lude was, so she did. He dug out his bottle and showed her, explaining that speed users always kept them nearby. "The beauty of 'em is, if you lude up and go too far, all you have to do is take some crank!"

She was a little reluctant, but he kept working on her until she accepted one. 'First one, and then, after it takes effect, I'll give you another,' Midget said to himself. 'Then you'll find out why the women like me so much. You'll be so horny you'll start beggin' me for it. Afterwards you won't be so fuckin' stuck-up any more.'

She was asking herself what in hell crank was when they heard a creak on the third step.

"Cats," Midget said, getting up to put some music on the boom box—another recent purchase. He opted for an old Modern Jazz Quartet tape he had found in somebody's car one night when he was checking doors in a parking garage. That had been a good day: the MJQ; three pairs of shades; a briefcase full of papers he had sold back to the owner, some idiot doctor, for $100; and a gas grill he was beginning to hope he wouldn't take to his grave. Somebody had to want it enough to meet his price.

Now that he was rich, it was time to dump his trophy collection.

"I love a kitty cat," Sammi drawled. She loved to hear the purr, and wondered why nobody ever used the beguiling sound as an undercurrent in a record. She could feel the dreaminess spreading though her like having syrup in her veins. Her sense of touch had thickened, and when Midget pulled his curtains shut the lower light made everything warm.

They just sat there for awhile. "I feel good," Sammi said. "I'll bet I can make a real good tape now."

"Forget the Melrose idea for the time being," Midget advised. "Let's you and me develop a brand new idea. Just the two of us, talkin' it through. Okay babe?"

"Whatever you say," she answered, tilting her head and smiling at how the room tilted too. It reminded her of one of those shake-up Irish Christmas scenes where the snow falls over and over again. But not exactly.

"Here's what I was thinkin'," Midget said, fiddling with a dirty thumb. "We need a tape where a beautiful young girl like you tells her lover how badly she needs to be fucked by him because her dopey husband can't get it up any more. Remember how we were talking about that before?" She didn't, but so what? "We could really score with a tape like that. Everyday at least two or three guys ask me about it. So let's just kind of talk it through once and then we'll go into the studio and record it. Okay?"

"I'll need a script," Sammi said.

"This'll be just a brainstorming session, Sammi. I'll take some notes and then we'll come up with a script for the actual recording. You ready for another lude yet?"

"I need some scripture," Sammi repeated, smiling. "Some acuscripture."

Glancing at the ceiling in frustration, Midget slowly repeated what he had just said. When it failed to register he tore some blank sheets off a notepad Tink had left there and handed them to her. "We'll fill it in as we go," he said. "Start with you tellin' me how dried-up your old man is, okay?"

"Okay," she said. Holding some paper in her hand was all she needed to get going. The way her vision was fluctuating in and out of synch, she probably would not have been able to read a script anyway.

"My husband's got a cock that's nothin' but a ... a worm," she said, laughing. "A night crawler! It crawls around at night, lookin' for a hole. But if it finds one, it's too weak to crawl in. It winds up climbing a tree and cuddling up in a bird's nest. A humming bird." She began to hum, and started clapping her hands to an imagined beat.

Midget wanted to slap her. "Is that why you need me to fuck you so bad, Sammi?" Midget asked, sliding his chair a little closer so he would be able to stroke her knee.

Stanley had finally reached the top step. His

breathing was labored and sweat was running down his brow from the tension. Yellow spots obscured his vision. Glad he had remembered his heart pills, he fished two out of their bottle. Their oblong shape seemed strange but he was sure he'd grabbed the right container so he swallowed them and refocused on listening to the voices in the room.

"Tell me you just married the old fart for his dough," Midget whispered.

Sammi repeated his words in a beguilingly innocent tone: "I just married the old fart for his do re mi. Fa so la. Ti. Dough." Wanting to sing, she repeated the notes.

"Tell me you really need me to fuck you good, to slip my long greasy cock into your pussy right now and make you feel like a woman again."

Laughing, Sammi did as she was told. The purring kitty was back, trying to tell her something important about the mysteries of life.

"Tell me again, with more feeling," Midget urged. So she did. "Tell me you'd do anything to get me to give you some cock. Make me believe it. Tell me you'll make your dried-up dirty old man give you all his money so you can give it to me. That way I won't have to worry about nothin' but givin' you the good cock you love."

Sammi cheerfully obeyed, fiddling with the bottle of pills Midget had put on the table.

"Tell me how, even if the old jerk could get it up, his

cock's so ugly you'd prob'ly puke just from seein' it," Midget began, feeling a stab of pleasure creep into his groin at last. 'Damn,' he told himself, 'I gotta record this.'

He would have continued but Stanley had heard more than he could stand. With his Colt in his hand he came though the door Midget had neglected to lock. Bursting into the kitchen, he was surprised to find them dressed— and her in the burgundy silk trousers for which he'd paid seven hundred dollars. But it didn't affect his reaction, which had been passed down to him from thousands of generations of cuckolded men: he aimed the shiny pistol at Midget and pulled the trigger. The force of the bullet lifted the small man off his chair and hurled him to the floor. Stanley's sense of accomplishment went through the roof.

"Hello, darling, you're home early, aren't you?" Sammi asked in a voice whose dreaminess echoed in her husband's ears even after his arm had swung mechanically to target its second victim and he had pulled the trigger again, nullifying the 19 months of what had been a generally blissful marriage. Nothing lasts forever.

Their blood mingled, Sammi's and Midget's, fulfilling the essence of the small man's long-harbored dream. It ran across the linoleum as if it had been given a mission by God Himself, sped its way over the living room's thin blood, and found the spot where Midget's floor hatch no longer fit because of the many pryings up. Letting gravity do its job, it waterfalled to the darkened grocery below, to which its hospitalized owner would not return. It pooled into the kind of perfect circle dictated by the golden mean, apt compensation for all the fluids that had gone up the pike in Midget's greedy hands, proving once again that the one great unrecognized force still afoot is the universe's unquenchable thirst for balance.

Spezio and the Carp had parked across the street and were just coming around the corner when they heard what their trained ears recognized as shots. Not very loud, but definitely gunshots. As pros they each drew their gun—a snub-nosed .38 for Spezio, a chrome .45 for his hulking soldier—and proceeded with cautious quickness up the stairs. Creak creak.

They could hear the music inside. Spezio winced; he had never liked jazz. Breathing heavily, the Carp went in first, standard policy for the junior. He was disarmed by what he saw: a small white-haired man kneeling on the floor to cradle a dead woman's head. Tears were running down the man's cheeks.

"Is that Sherri?" the Carp asked.

"You dirty swine!" Stanley answered. The gun in his hand went off, almost as if it had a will of its own. The bullet hit the huge man squarely in the chest, tilting him back into Spezio. He would take that as a no.

Carpenter's life flashed before his eyes. He saw his illiterate laborer father, who had been crushed in a so-called accident at his job, and his alcoholic mother, a fat slob who had never told him the truth and had done her best to trick him out of everything he had ever earned until he broke her nose and slammed the door for good. He pictured the kids he had gone to school with until he quit in disgust, the boys he had beaten up simply to demonstrate his one talent and the girls who had ridiculed him as 'lardo' or 'blockhead' as they laughed and flexed their knees on a swing, provoking him into applying their image to the anonymous rented girls he had sampled and abandoned as he made his way to the end.

He remembered Pansy O'Toole, the first woman he had slept with without having to pay, and how she had sternly ordered him afterwards not to ever say anything to anyone. He had understood: she would have been humiliated if her friends found out. Enraged, he had knocked her out with one punch—another first. In retrospect, everything seemed tainted. Even the money he had made with Spezio. He'd had to let himself be ridiculed whenever something went wrong, without ever answering back. The long-planned revenge against his boss, culminating in a triumphal statement he had revised for years would have to come in a different life.

All in all, his spirit was glad to leave such an ungainly and ill-equipped body. Its occupation of this flesh had been one long embarrassment. Maybe it would have better luck on the next go around. One could only hope.

Stanley fired twice again, aiming at the second man, but Carpenter's mass proved an impenetrable shield, giving Spezio all the time he needed to send his own bullet straight into the crying old man's grief-addled brain. Sweet Lou would have to find another partner to swindle and crush.

The kitchen was a sea of bodies. The smoke was chokingly thick. Spezio stepped over the dead carefully until he could see that the woman was not Sherri. Then he cursed, wiped his prints from his .38, and traded guns with the Carp, automatically squeezing his still-flexible fingers around the handle and holding them there while he looked around the room. It never hurt to blame a dead man, he thought. Many noble careers had been built on this sound principle.

He saw the pills, and the tape with 'Aberdeen, rough cut' penciled on its label. He saw the dirty dishes piled in the sink, the new but already grime-covered stove and refrigerator, and some of the electronics in the living room. The marigolds Alice had brought had withered and died. Once she gave up on the business there had been no one to water them.

There was no Sherri. Damn!

He let the Carp's gnarly hand drop to the floor and prowled through the apartment, looking for clues to her whereabouts. It was easy for him to locate the records Tink had stashed in an end table. He found copies of the ads Midget had placed in various newspapers, a torn straight-jacket costume drooped over a chair, awaiting repair, and the supply of tapes they had accumulated for sale or use. But there were no pictures, and nothing bearing Sherri's name.

He decided he would just have to wait. He'd come this far. He dragged the four bodies into the living room, one by one. Panting, he repeated an often-made promise to himself: 'I gotta start working out.' Seeing the .38, he kicked it to where the Carp might conceivably have dropped it in the living room. Then he took out one of his imported cigars.

Carpenter's body called for a fire. He was sure of that. The man was too large to move, and Spezio did not want his cohort to be identified. There could be ways to explain Carpenter's presence: "He must've been runnin' his own game; I could kick myself now for not having picked up on the signs"—but he didn't want to have to. Besides, there was something purifying about a good blaze. And fate agreed: a can of gas was sitting beneath a rusty backyard grill.

Maybe it was time to retire, he thought, drifting into the kitchen. Leaning against the counter for a deep drag of Cuban smoke, he gave himself a moment's pleasure by running though his fantasy of life in the Caribbean again. Ah, those sexy little native bunnies, he thought. They will do anything for a few American dollars.

He knew he had to stay calm but did not have enough information about this operation to know for how long. He checked the fridge—luckily, it was packed with beer, but unluckily it was not his brand. Turning off the abominable music, he sat down to wait. Maybe he would pick up a girl from Negril, take her out in his boat, and tell her she would have to convince him not to make her swim to shore. Without her swimsuit. Once again this reliable daydream made him hard, and when he was hard, nothing else mattered. The world was aglow with promise.

As it turned out, he did not have long to wait. He was nearing the end of his cigar and asking himself if he were making any mistakes when he heard steps on the stairs. He stepped into the living room and stood behind the archway to make sure that whoever opened the door came all the way in.

He was in luck—in a sense. Gina and Tink were returning from their engagement in Waterville. As soon as she opened the door she inhaled the gunfire stench and recognized the blood on the floor. She tried to stop, but the ungainly Tink always climbed stairs as if they were an obstacle course and his lumbering momentum carried both of them into the room.

Spezio stepped out, smiling coldly. "Hello, Sherri," he greeted her.

"Richard! Boy am I glad to see you," she said, able to mask her surprise even though she felt her lunch dissolve in her the ruthless blender which her gut had become.

"I'll just bet," Spezio spit out, letting his stub fall to the floor.

"What's going on?" Tink demanded, his eyes doing

pinwheels. Spezio did not even bother to look; Tink was someone it was easy to ignore. Tink repeated his question, adding, "Why'd he call you Sherri?" But she too ignored him. She was thinking fast—no time to stop the train for an unticketed passenger.

"How'd you manage to find me?" she asked.

"I just peed off a mountain and watched which way it ran," he told her, delighted at her lack of comprehension.

"You can't talk to her like that." Tink warned.

"Or what, fat boy?" Spezio challenged, flicking his gun.

Tink looked at Gina for support but she was focused on Spezio. "So, what're you doin' here?" she asked.

"Your fuckhead husband found out where you were. He'll be here tomorrow. I made sure I got here first."

"You're married?" Tink asked.

"Thanks for the warning," Gina told Spezio, putting as much warmth as she could into her words. "I better head south. I guess I was crazy to come this close to home."

She turned and took a step toward the door, but Spezio said, "Not so fast, Sherri. If he found you once, he'll find you again. I can't have that."

She turned back and came up to within a few feet of him. She was well aware of the danger—his pillow talk had been a recitation of brutal crimes. "Why don't you talk him out of trying to find me?" she said, touching his chest lightly with two fingers. "You oughta know how. Tell him in a way he can't shrug off. I'll send you a postcard when I get to where I'm going."

"It's not so simple anymore," he said, fighting off the nostalgia induced by her voice. "C'mon in the other room."

She did as he asked. He used his gun to motion for Tink to follow, and he followed Tink. The stench of death was overwhelming. When Tink saw the four bodies he started to shake. Then a spasm began to work its way through him, making him sink to his knees and go into dry heaves. He was no longer in a comic book world.

"You see what happened here," Spezio said calmly.

"Looks like they all shot each other," Gina replied. "Well, shit happens."

"You're good, I've gotta hand it to you. But I can't have anybody out there knowin' I was even here. I'm sorry, Sherri, but I just wouldn't be able to sleep. If there was any other way...."

He raised Carpenter's gun, the chrome 45.

"Shit, Richard, we've always been a team," Gina wheedled.

"I know. That's what makes this so damn hard. But

some things just gotta be done."

Spezio stood there, aiming his gun at her, his eyes misting. He shook his head, and then took a deep breath, resolving to do what he knew he had to. On his hands and knees on the floor, trying to control his retching, Tink saw the snub-nose .38. He had not fired a gun since he was a kid but he told himself there was no time like the present to break the string. He rode out another bout of convulsions, shifting to put his body between Spezio and the gun on the floor. Moving slowly, he slipped his finger around the trigger, basking in the warmth of anticipating how Gina would look at him when he saved her. He had no idea if the gun was loaded but would find out soon enough. He counted to three and rolled onto his back to fire up at the man standing behind him, just like he'd seen on TV.

He never had a chance. Spezio, a true pro, shot him in the head when he was half-way through his roll. Tink fell across Midget's body with a soft groan, although some of his brains hit the floor beyond, and even the far wall.

"Now there's nobody to tell," Gina said. The roar of the gun echoed in her ears.

"Almost nobody," he said, turning his gun toward her.

He began to squeeze the trigger but was stopped by an unexpected voice from the kitchen: "Shootin' fish in a barrel, eh, Richard?" It was Gus Litwak, who had slipped into the apartment unnoticed and had calmed the turmoil in his stomach by dropping one of the antacids sitting in an unmarked vial on the kitchen table.

"Darling!" Gina called to him. "Thank God you made it!"

"They knew you were coming," Spezio said, so surprised that he lowered his gun and turned to face him. "They set you up, amigo. It's lucky we got wind of it."

"Is that right?" Gus said, mocking his attempt at camaraderie with the coolness of his tone. "Your buddy the Carp don't look so lucky."

"He died on your behalf," Spezio said. "Just ask Sherri."

Gus's eyes darted to his wife. It was the chance Spezio was waiting for. He raised the .45 again and tried to fire, but Carp's gun was heavier than what he was used to and Gus dropped him before he could get his shot off. Spezio cursed the idiotic Carpenter's choice of weaponry as he fell, a taunting voice in the back of his head saying, 'I'll bait the hook for you, honey, while you open us fresh cold ones'. Ah, such sweet, sweet mockery. Zooming out over the tumultuous blue-green sea, his joyful freed animus never felt its empty body hit the floor.

Gina screamed and ran toward her husband, saying, "Oh thank God! He was gonna kill me and then wait for you to show up and kill you too!" The reverberating echo of the gunshot fractured her reality into the shards of a smashed mirror.

"That's far enough," Gus said, stopping her approach with a wave of his gun. There was something wrong with him, she thought; it was as if he were dazed, not quite himself.

"So, Sherri," he said, speaking from a great distance. She saw that he needed a shave. "How've you been?" he asked.

"Terrible! These people captured me on my way back to see you to try to make it right between us. They held me prisoner and made me do all sorts of horrible things."

A funny little smile played briefly over his lips. Spots appeared before his eyes that he tried to blink away. "But you managed to enjoy it anyway, didn't you," he said.

"I tried to make the best of it. They were sick, Gus," she said. "I never knew if I'd see you again. What else could I do? As far as I'm concerned, they got what they deserve."

He had started to sweat. Something was happening to his world: its continuity was dissolving into a sequence of rigid frames, as if he were becoming the nude descending. He wiped his brow jerkily with the sleeve on the arm with which he held his gun. "Do you want to tell me about it, Sherri?" he asked, squinting in her direction. He had been schooled on the importance of the rite of final confession.

"If you'd like," she said in a subdued voice. She turned so she was standing at about a 30° angle, put her hands together, and started to talk in a low, sing-songy voice. It had worked on several angry men, convincing them to get over it and pay up to go again. "They, uh, had this sex-enhancing costume, Gus, that they asked me to put on. I didn't want to but they made me. You know how you could always get me to do anything you wanted once you got me real hot? You remember that?"

He tilted his head a little by way of answering.

"Well, I didn't think that just a costume would make me feel that way, but it did. It was, uh, like a fake straight-jacket. It didn't have a strap across my clit or anything, like you might imagine. Know what I mean? That would rub it, like you used to do—remember? This just made me feel like I was powerless so I didn't have to worry about anyone sayin' I was a cheap slut who only wanted to fuck or nothin'."

She could tell he was not focusing properly. Her guess was sleep deprivation or maybe some new virus had invaded his system. She increased her syncopation and adopted a more emotional tone. She turned, reducing the angle between them.

"You ever hear of something like that? I mean, in your work, or anything?" she asked. She was starting to get a little of her self-confidence back.

He shook his head and wiped his brow again. His forehead looked clammy and pale.

"So I put this costume on, and they played a tape. Of dirty talkin'? They just sat there grinnin', not sayin' anything. Just lettin' the dirty talkin' and the costume work on me. I've always been a sucker for that kinda stuff. They turned the lights down and put some music on in the background. I kept thinkin', 'they're crazy if they think this is gonna work on me'."

She took a step, not closer to Gus but maintaining the same distance, as if she were held by a string. A bright moon circling a dark planet. She moved toward the archway to the kitchen to get away from the stink of death.

"One of 'em says to me, 'Honey, you can just tell us whatever you're thinkin'. Whatever comes to your mind.' So I thought I'd fool 'em by makin' somethin' up, see. I started tellin' 'em that it was workin', that I could feel a tingle in my thighs. Like somebody was rubbin' me with a vibrator, you know what I mean? Remember how you used to get me all worked up? Once I'd said it I kind of actually began to feel it, see. Movin' it back and forth on my thighs, gettin' closer and closer to my pussy. Teasin' me, wantin' me to tell them, 'Just go ahead, touch my clit a little with it, okay?'"

She had reached the kitchen. Gus had turned as she went past him to keep her in his sight. She surveyed the dimmer room quickly, hoping there might be something there she could use to defend herself. "It was like a little fire was startin' to burn in my groin," she continued, feeling more sure of herself. "You ever have that happen to you? I mean, you kind of know it's silly and all, but there it is. You're sort of caught up in a thick, good feeling. I said to myself, 'I shouldn't be doin' this', but, on the other hand since I was wearin' this fake costume and all I thought, 'Well, it ain't really my fault. There's nothin' I can do so I might as well enjoy it.' Know what I mean? You ever been in that kinda deal?"

When she glanced back over her shoulder Gus nodded awkwardly on cue, like a horse trying to count. One plus two, clomp clomp clomp. She saw the torn costume dangling over a chair. She noticed a tape in the boom box, which gave her hope. She pushed the play button, saying, "I wonder if this is the one. Just listen, you'll see what I mean." She was disappointed when the music of the MJQ filtered into the room, muted but full of extravagance and surprise.

Whoever was operating Gus's personal time machine was on a bender.

"That's how they got control over me, Gus," she told him, speaking low and earnestly and pushing her gaze into his skull. Tentacles of mind power—so fulfilling to exercise. "Under the right circumstances their costume let me get hotter than I'd ever been before. Except when I was with you, I mean. It was like when I put it on, I was free to feel things more deeply. One of them explained how we got all these pressures on us. We can tell ourselves we're gonna ignore them, but we can't.

They're part of our world. 'They're subliminal,' the guy said; 'we can't tune 'em out.' We need to override them with a more powerful symbol, like the release you get from their outfit. These costumes really work! By making us think we have no choice, they set us free. Nothin' to lose means go for broke, right? You believe me, don't you? I wouldn't lie at a time like this."

Gus shook his head. He took a few wobbly steps into the kitchen and leaned back against the sink. He pointed his gun at the floor.

"It's true," she asserted, allowing a smile to flicker across her lips. "They work on anyone. A man or a woman. Whoever puts one on gets this tingly, wonderful feeling. I know it sounds crazy, but it's true. Once they got me started wearin' one, they could get me to do anything they wanted. I used to wear one to bed and have these delicious dreams in which you and I were doing our three-pillow trick. If they had said, 'You're free to go but you gotta leave the costume', I probably would have stayed. Just thinkin' of how it feels is kind of exciting me, even right now. You want a beer or anything, Gus?"

He shook his head but she ignored him and took two beers from the fridge. She opened them and handed one to him, which he took with his free hand. Remembering how she had always been able to bend him to her will gave her hope.

There was a stack of tapes on the counter across from the sink. She moved over to them to scan their labels for

You Know What I Like, which they all considered Sammi's masterpiece. She hoped it was there; she did not want to go back into the living room under any circumstances.

She was in luck: there it was. "I think this is the first tape they made me listen to," she said, taking a cassette player from the wall cabinet, popping Sammi's tape in, and turning it on. Then she lowered the volume on the boom box to make the music retreat into the background. The MJQ would not have minded playing second fiddle to good slut talk at all.

Sammi's rhythmic voice wafted into the room: "You know what I like, which is to do anything that will please you. I just want to excite you, and get you so worked up that you'll think about me all the time and have me come over and do all the things that give you pleasure. That's what I really enjoy. I just want to do whatever I can to excite you, because that's what excites me. That's the only thing I really want."

Gus seemed a little disoriented. He put his can of beer on the table even though he had barely taken a sip, and leaned back against the sink again. His eyes were flitting around the room like trapped bees, and his face had beaded up with sweat. He kept smiling impishly, and then forcing himself to look stern again. She thought he was losing it.

When Sammi paused Sherri filled the void. "I found myself thinking, 'This is ridiculous; it won't hurt me to play along.' But even as I told myself it was nothing, it was worming its way under my skin. Why don't you stick your gun in your belt or something while I'm explaining this to you. You know you're so much stronger than me that you could take me with one hand tied behind your back."

She turned around and opened the wall cabinet, thinking there was a greater chance of him complying if she didn't look. Holding her breath, she fiddled in the cabinet for a moment and then turned back. But he still had his gun in his hand.

She forced herself to stay calm. "Go ahead and stick it in your belt so I can show you one of the costumes," she told him, turning back to the cabinet and rummaging in it. She pulled out a leopard-skin straight-jacket and turned back to him. He was still holding his gun. "This is the baby," she said, unfolding it as she crossed the room toward him. When she handed him the outfit he took it with his left hand, supporting it with his gun as well to keep it from dangling on the floor. She thought she was half-way home.

"It don't look like nothin' special, does it," she said.

He shook his head.

"But it works. Almost like magic. On a woman or a man. Really! I can prove it, too. I wouldn't have believed it but it works! Shit, Gus, I'll bet it would even work on you. That would be the ultimate test, right, 'cause you're so strong-minded."

He had it in his hands, but kept looking at her. Smiling knowingly, she backed away from him to give him a chance to examine it, and turned down Sammi's tape so it joined the MJQ as a second element of the background. When she moved away, he gave the costume a quick glance.

"I guess I must be hooked on it, 'cause just seein' it and touchin' it's got me real wet," she told him, turning down the overhead light. "Want me to model it for you?"

His eyes widened a bit, so she came forward again and took it from him, brushing against him in the process. She discreetly rolled the sleeves back, and then slipped it over her head. Once she had wiggled into it, she put her arms behind her back, turning her hands so the Velcro strips would not mesh.

"Maybe it's because I've been trained, but I really get off wearin' this," she told him, trying to match her tone to Sammi's. "Remember how you used to like fuckin' me when I'd get on top? God, you made me feel like I was a buckin' bronco you could get galloping all over the corral. I used to come so much that it almost split me open. I never told you how good it was, but you knew I couldn't get enough of you. It's just too bad Spezio got involved. He forced me to do some things against my will but each time, I just closed my eyes and thought about you. He said he'd take you out if I didn't go along and I believed him. He was a vicious, evil, creep, and he wound up costing me the best thing I ever had. I did that shit to save your life, Gus. Honest I did. My life turned to crap after that and I had to take off, but I was tryin' to get back to you, Gus, the whole time, so I could get some more of your good fuckin'. Ever since I met you it's the only thing I've wanted. You gotta believe me."

She came over to him and leaned against him. "Just give me one little kiss while I'm all bound up like this," she said enticingly, rubbing against him, seeking his lips with hers. He brushed his mouth against hers, but then turned his head.

"Oh, I think I'm gonna come, if you'd just do that one more time," she said, seeking his lips again. When he gave her a second brief kiss she began to moan. She rubbed her body against him more energetically, and simulated a mild orgasm by rolling her eyes upwards. Then she wilted and drifted back to the opposite counter where she stood panting.

After a minute she brought her hands out from behind her back, and then pulled the straight-jacket off over her head. "God damn that was good! But I suppose it was at least partially this outfit. Let's try it on you once," she said in a definitive tone. "No harm in that, right?" At that moment her gut had become so brittle it could have splintered into a thousand pieces if he said the wrong word.

She approached him again, leering seductively. She spread the gathered-up material with both hands and raised it to slip over his head. To her surprise and tremendous relief, he ducked his head just a little and put his hands forward to insert them in the sleeves. The gun came through first; then his hands. She began to breathe more easily.

She stepped back and pulled the garment over him. "God, it even turns me on just seein' you like this," she said, her eyes squeezed into slits. "I think I'm gonna come again! This is like a dream."

His hands at his sides, he looked down at the spotted fabric, mesmerized by its unfamiliarity.

"Stick your gun in your belt, and cross your arms over your stomach," she told him. "That's safe enough, isn't it? Let's see if this is enough to make you come, okay? You know you're the only man I ever loved."

He stared at her for a moment before doing as she said.

"God, you're sexy," she said. "Let's give it a few minutes to work since this is your first time. Damn it, though, just seein' you like this is gettin' me all turned on again. You were the best I ever had, Gus. The best by far. I hope you never doubted that."

He stood there dumbly, blinking, a half smile forming and unforming on his lips.

She knew she had reached the critical point. She had to be utterly careful. She had almost won, but it could still blow up in her face. Breathing more heavily, she said she thought that if she kissed him she would have such an orgasm that she would not be able to stand. "Don't move, I'm gonna give you one dynamite kiss, okay? This could put us both over the edge."

She crossed over to him again, slowly, and leaned against him. "You're really the only man I ever fucked," she murmured. "Everybody else was just a stand-in for you. The only way I could tolerate them was by pretending they were you."

Grinding against him, slowly and sinuously, she brought her mouth closer to his. She brushed his cheek with her lips as she felt along his arms for the ends of the still-rolled-up cuffs. "You're ready to come, aren't you, Gus," she whispered, slowly tugging at the sleeve ends. "That's really why you came down to Toledo, isn't it. Your cock is leading you around. This is gonna be sensational for both of us, don't you think? This could be the best ever. I don't know if I can wait, honey, it's starting already, I don't think I can hold back, ugh ... Ugh ... UGH!"

She leaned into him harder and moaned loudly, yanking the rolled-up cuffs over his hands and pulling the sleeve ends together behind his back. Once they touched she pressed the Velcro strips to secure the straight-jacket. Then she stepped back and slapped him as hard as she could across the face to chase away his dopey look. She took his gun out of his belt as he struggled to break free. She felt the same flush of victory as a rodeo hand gets from hog-tying an unruly calf.

She stepped back to survey her handiwork, saying, "Well well well. You always were a sucker for a little sweet talk, Gus."

Chapter 15

Gus struggled mightily against his bonds, which only set them more tightly. Sneering, Gina watched him from across the room while she poured herself a stiff drink. When he finally realized the futility of his efforts and gave up she taunted him, saying, "Whatever am I gonna do with you, Gus, to keep you from fuckin' me over?"

He glared at her in silence, his eyes wild with rage.

"Am I gonna have to shoot you to get you off my back?" she asked, carelessly brandishing his gun.

He did not reply.

"You know, this whole thing really is that asshole Spezio's fault," she went on, finishing her drink and putting the glass down. "He got me involved in a sting when Sheila backed out. Remember that bitch? I hate her guts. Of course the extra money was nice. You never gave me very much. But he couldn't keep his hands off me. I'm glad you shot the jerk."

She paused for a moment before adding, "I really did like you, Gus, but I suppose we're way past that now."

She was going to continue but she heard a creak on the stairs. Keeping the gun on Gus, she went to the door and pulled the curtain aside. Tony was coming up the steps.

Flashing the gun at Gus to keep him in place, she opened the door a crack and called down, "Hey, you got your car?"

"I need to talk to you, Gina," Tony said.

"Have you got your car?" she repeated so harshly he froze in his tracks.

"Well, yes ...."

"Go get it, and park at the bottom of the stairway, okay? I need you to help me. I'll be out in about 20 minutes."

He was going to say something but changed his mind and retreated down the steps. She closed the door and returned her attention to her former husband.

"I think you deserve the full experience, Gus," she told him. "So you know what I've had to go through. First, there's the blindfold."

She set the gun down, took a roll of surgical tape from the supplies cabinet, and went over to him. He pulled his head away, though, when she tried to wrap him.

"I could just shoot you," she told him.

That made him more docile. She wrapped the tape around his head so it covered his eyes, and used Midget's felt tips to draw new eyes, making them wide and blue with crude black lashes. She found one of the wigs they had used with their mannequin and taped that on his head as well. He did not make a pretty girl.

She noticed the Aberdeen tape next to the bottle of Midget's pills. That gave her an idea. She took it into the living room where she put it in Tink's machine to listen to. Where Poppy said, "Please remove my blindfold," she erased it, leaving a blank section.

Then she ran it to the end, backed up a little, and added a final command, dropping her voice as low as she could to approximate Poppy's androgynous tone: "Thanks for the wonderful treatment. I really loved it. I feel I'm half way to a great new life, and I owe it all to you. But could you do me one more favor, please? I'll really appreciate it. I could use a little more of this wonderful treatment. It's helping me find my true self, you know? Would you run this tape back to the beginning and drive me over to one of your friends? I know they won't be as satisfying as you, but it'll be really good for me to get a little more. Thanks a lot. I'll never forget you and your special touch."

She put the edited tape in one of their miniaturized players and strapped the player around Gus's neck. Seeing Midget's pills and knowing what they did, she decided to feed a couple to Gus to make everything go smoothly. She told him they were darvons which she wanted him to take in order to relax. She popped two in his mouth and held a glass of water up and made him swallow. Three would last him all night.

She took a hollow plastic ball from the cabinet,

pushed it into his mouth, and taped it in. Then she peeled a set of garish lips from its waxy backer and stuck them over the surgical tape. Finally she looked up Donald Farrington's number in the file and gave him a call.

"We've arranged a visitation for you," she said. "Could you be ready to receive in about a half hour? The person we're sending you is very special."

"Uh, well I had ... uh, yes, I suppose so," the old fruit replied, his pulse rate notably increasing.

There was one more thing to do. Every time they'd divvied up the money she had listened to Midget surreptitiously squirrel his share away. She couldn't help it; it was only natural. She had pretty much determined that his hiding place was in the end table in the living room, next to the stolen grill. She went to it and yanked the drawer out and peered into its hole. Sure enough, there was a cardboard folder at the back, thumb-tacked to the inside. She reached in and pulled out wads of money, which she stuffed into her purse.

After wiping off her prints she dropped the gun on the pile of bodies, and then explained to the mute Gus that she would be taking him from the apartment and down the stairs. "So watch your step, okay?"

He nodded, resigned. He was floating way above the bull shit now. He was somewhere out in a boat, writing his book. She took a last look around to see if there was anything else she wanted. She decided not.

Outside it was just getting dark. The bound and blindfolded man was surprisingly clumsy so she motioned for Tony, who was watching from his car. He came halfway up the stairs but when he started to speak she barked at him, "Shhh! Don't say a thing!"

The two of them got Gus into the back seat, but she had another idea and ran back up the stairs. "I won't be a minute," she said over her shoulder, thinking of the red-and-yellow can.

When she returned she directed Tony to drive toward Farrington's large brick home in Aberdeen. He wanted to warn her about the police but each time he started to speak she shook him off. After a few blocks she had another brainstorm. "What was the name of that guy you hated?" she asked Tony. "You know, the guy you were setting up when we met."

"Bob Arkin. Why?"

"Head for his house," she ordered. "We might as well tie up all the loose ends."

Tony wasn't sure at first, but he did as she said. Obeying her gave him the wrath of complicity. The closer they got to Bob's, the more he realized what she planned and the happier he became. When they entered Vinewood and parked in front of the familiar bungalow he could not suppress a grin.

It took both of them to transpose the bound and gagged Gus Litwak to Bob's unassuming stoop. Across the street the renegade black cat was too engrossed in licking its left front paw to notice. Back in Tony's car, Gina called Bob on the cell phone Tink had given her—the last of his gifts. Adopting her sexiest voice, she said, "I'm back, darling. Right outside your door. This is going to be extra special, honey. I want you to turn off your lights and put on some of that great music of yours before you let me in. I'm really horny. I'm hotter than I've ever been. Take me right into your bedroom, okay. I want you to be a little rougher this time. I've been dreaming about the mother of all orgasms. Just push me down on my tummy, okay, and start feeding me your beautiful cock. I want this to be an experience neither one of us ever forgets. Darling, I can't wait any longer. Please hang up and do me right now! I'll be so grateful."

She clicked the phone off, and grinned at Tony. "Could I use it?" he asked. "I'd like to call Ray and tell him the news."

When they were heading for her apartment on Basswood Street, Gina told Tony that now he could tell her why he showed up at Midget's apartment.

"I wanted to let you know the cops were close to figuring out your operation," he said, hepped up about finally getting his revenge on Bob..

"So you came to warn me. How sweet," she chided. "Or maybe you were just worried that if they caught me they might find out how you got me started."

He was a little rattled. "No, I swear!" he replied.

"Don't worry," she told him. "I'm leaving town. I just want to get some things from my apartment. I'm gonna head west. Ohio is too fuckin' provincial."

"Where are gonna go?"

"I don't know. I've heard great things about California."

They drove along in silence until Gina asked Tony why he stuck around Toledo.

"Why not?"

"Because you got a shit job, no friends, and no regular pussy. Hey, why don't you come with me?"

"I couldn't do that," he said automatically. But the way she was looking at him put it into doubt. The only way to get off the train to nowhere was to step through the door.

"Yes you could," she told him.

There was such certainty in her voice that his face began to tingle. When they came to Elm Street he hit the brake and stopped. "Well, we should turn here," he said. "My place is on Grant, on the way to yours. We should get my stuff first."

"Atta boy!" she replied, smiling.

She took a shower in Tony's bathroom while he packed his things. He was compelled to call TKD and deliver his resignation. When the surprised clerk asked him for a reason, he told her, "You've got too many punk-butts there for my taste."

"Pardon me?" the woman replied.

"Like Bob Arkin," Tony calmly stated. "Don't tell me you didn't know."

Everything he owned except his collection of model Civil War soldiers fit into the trunk of his car, and that was something he was ready to leave behind. Then it was off to her apartment. She told him to wait, but took the keys, just in case.

She was back in ten minutes with two suitcases and a hat box, which she threw in the back seat. As he pulled away she turned his rear-view mirror toward herself and reapplied her make-up. He kept stealing glances at her, and never saw the plumes of smoke spiraling up from Midget's apartment ten blocks behind. One of the things she had shared with Spezio was a belief in the purification of fire.

They left Toledo at 10:30, driving out along the river on Highway 24. Tony remarked that he had not had supper yet but she refused to let him stop until they crossed into Indiana shortly after midnight. It was the beginning of her giving the orders. "You know, we're lucky we got out when we did," she said. "If we kept it going I think we would have instigated a real revolution. Sooner or later people were going to start recording their own tapes—for every aspect of their lives. Going to work; talking with their spouse; even ordering a meal.

That way instead of taking the risk of venturing something personal they could simply push play and avoid all responsibility. The era of spontaneous conversation would come to an end!"

They skirted Fort Wayne and continued on 24 to Marion, where they switched to 37. Soon it was just them and the truckers. She took a quick nap, lulled by the constant motion, and awoke much refreshed. A full moon had come out, bathing them with a dim, eerie light.

"I don't have a lot of money," Tony remarked, holding them at 60. "I'll have to look for a job. I'm not worried, though. Somebody's bound to be hiring."

"Didn't I tell you?" she teased. "You're gonna work for me now."

"What? Doin' what? Not the same business you were in back in Toledo."

"Hell no! You had that whole gimmick backwards! I got a better deal worked out. Let me show you," she told him, reaching back over the seat for her hat box. This was something she had put a lot of thought into and had been working on for some time.

His eyes hungrily took in the way her stretching pulled her blouse tight against her breast. He couldn't wait until they stopped for the night. "Look at this," she said, pulling out a kind of leather aviator's helmet. "Tink helped me rig this up. It's got those new flat Bose speakers in the ear flaps, a miniature cassette player in the back. And a little lock right here, see. So you can't get it off unless I let you."

"What the heck?"

"Let me show you how it works," she said.

"That's okay," he replied, pulling away.

"No, I insist," she said. "See, the whole point of this biz is to get a man turned on. Hell, the sex itself is nothin'. Anybody can have all the sex he wants. Or almost anybody. But if it ain't exciting, it just ain't any good. Right?"

He nodded like an incipient zombie.

"You had a fair idea with your straight-jacket routine, but you didn't take it far enough. This is much better. This little gizmo puts the message right inside the guy's head. I don't have to do nothin', or hardly nothin', with this thing going, see. Let me put it on you, just for a demonstration. After all, helpin' me with this business is gonna be your new job. You got a lot to learn, but we're gonna make a real good team."

He didn't want to but she insisted, so he reluctantly tilted his head for her to slip the device on, hoping that maybe then she'd let him find them a motel. She buckled it tightly and snapped the lock, and asked how it felt. But he could not quite make out what she said.

Satisfied, she took a remote control from the box,

aimed it at the helmet, and pushed the 'play'. A woman's rich, sensual voice—not Sammi's, but Gina's own—wafted into his ears. "You really are a big sexy guy," the voice cooed, filling his head. "I'll bet you know all the tricks a woman likes, and love to perform them," it continued. "I can tell you get off just from givin' a woman pleasure, don't you. That's what men are for, right? And you're a real man. I think you're my kind of guy, and I'm gonna give you a chance to prove it."

She could sense his eyes misting over as he darted glances at her. "I hope you're not in any hurry," her recorded voice was almost singing. The way it reverberated through him made him feel he was closer to her than he had ever been to a woman. He wanted to take special steps to please her. "Anything worth doin' is worth doin' right, honey," it continued. "I want you to take your time, because I've got all night."

He was beginning to drool, but she ignored him. Now that he was under control, she could make some plans. 'I should have him buy me a bicycle shop,' she told herself. 'Those funny helmets would be a good place to start. And maybe a hearing aid store, if I can get the equipment miniaturized. Point, click, and smile; this's gonna be great. After all, what I wanna tell guys is only what they really want to hear: to please a woman all they have to do is whatever she says.'

So it turned out she was ready to start a revolution in sexual mores after all.

www.ingramcontent.com/pod-product-compliance
Lightning Source LLC
Chambersburg PA
CBHW020555180626
46810CB00007B/2516